M K Indira
The Young Widow

Translated from Kannada
by Tejaswini Niranjana

Livewire Books for Teenagers
Published by The Women's Press Limited 1991
A member of the Namara Group
34 Great Sutton Street, London EC1V ODX

First published as Phaniyamma by
Kali for Women 1990
A 36 Gulmohar Park, New Delhi 110049, India

British Library Cataloguing in Publication Data
Indira, M. K.
    The young widow: a novel. — (Livewire).
    I. Title   II. Series   III [Phaniyamma. English]
    894.81437

    ISBN 0-7043 4926-4

Typeset by AKM Associates (UK) Ltd, Southall
Printed and bound in Great Britain by BPCC Hazell Books
Aylesbury, Bucks, Member of BPCC Ltd

Thanks to
Anupama Niranjana
Seemanthini Niranjana
Shivarama Padikkal
and Ashok Dhareshwar
for help with these words.

Epigraph

She was green
She grew warm
    this sapling of a girl
    who knew no lies

She became a song
She ripened
    this girl turned to dust
    turned into a memory
    into sorrow, into a story
    hiding all in her heart

Ambikatanayadatta

One

Born in 1840, died in 1952; she seemed to have lived an ordinary life. Those who lived with her did not know her innermost secrets. Only Banashankari remained to tell the story of her life, and pass it on to her daughters.

This writer's grandfather Shanbhag Kittappa used to say that no other woman like his sister Phani had ever been born or would be in the future. The only thing the children knew was that all madi women were the same. They ate once a day, and had a snack at night!

Since, I, Banashankari's daughter Indi, had heard Phaniyamma's story from my mother, and had actually seen Ancheyatthe myself, I was able to write this little history. Although this is the story of a nameless widow, it seemed to me that there was something of significance here. Which is why this book was written.

It was perhaps around 1840. No one remembers now which year it was. One night, in the season of Aashaada, Sannamma, the wife of Anchetamayya of Hebbalige, went into labour. That wasn't an unusual thing either.

Anchemane, or the Postal House, was a big title in the days of the British. Tamayya's dwelling was traditionally known as 'Anchemane'. It was a house with sixteen pillars, an open courtyard in the centre, and a tiled roof. In the village of Hebbalige, which had only five Brahmin households, Tamayya's was the biggest house and the only one with tiles. The other four were roofed with dried grass.

Neither the inhabitants of Anchemane nor their neighbours knew how many people lived in the Postal House. In

1

those days it was a sin and a crime to count how many people or how many children there were.

Tamayya's father had eighteen or twenty children. The house was always full of children, grandchildren, great grandchildren, visitors, sons-in-law and daughters-in-law.

A house in the Malnad hills. Near Tirthahalli. In the rich earth were grain fields, and gardens, for sugarcane, banana, coconut, vegetables, fruits, and flowers. There were more cattle than people. The servants and farm-hands lived in separate houses about a furlong away.

In those times the concept of *madi* was cherished, which gave special place to that which was sacred or 'pure'. Along with *madi* went the upholding of tradition, ritual and above all the attitude of frogs-in-a-well. If anything happened in a neighbouring village which went against tradition, there was an uproar. Through the people of the Anchemane the news would spread to all the surrounding villages in less than a fortnight. Then the Brahmins would have to gird up their dhotis and walk the thirty miles to Sringeri. The head-priest was Sri Sri Sri Nrsimhabharathiswamigalavaru then. Ex-communication was a dreaded and frequent punishment. A child widow, for instance, who became pregnant. The man who impregnated her would go himself to Sringeri and procure the order for her excommunication. The head-priest, of course, was celibate, a *sanyasi*, who did not realize that it was a blot on his chastity to listen to all these tales of profligacy. With a wave of his hand he entrusted the decision to the religious officials of the temple, and they were like wolves left to guard a flock of sheep. As soon as a few genuine silver rupees were nestling in the fold of their dhotis the poor widow's fate was sealed.

At a time when laws more terrible than these were in force, our heroine was born to Sannamma, wife of Tamayya. It was no big event. Every month at least two births took place in that house. And our heroine was one of fifteen brothers and sisters. The house was full of old women, and someone or the other would play midwife. It was no big thing to bear a child. Whether a woman was sick or pregnant, she had to work hard all day, until her body drooped with fatigue. Only when she felt the first pains could she go into the birthing room, where everything would be ready—a gunny bag, a blanket, an earthen jar for the rubbish, betel leaf and nut, musk, the cap for the new mother, a *mora* for the child to be lain in.

Before that there would be an old man in the doorway, holding an hour-glass. During the day they told the time by the sun's shadow on the wall. But in the rainy season the sun does not show its face in the Malnad for many months, and then you need an hour-glass. Or if it's night. This hour-glass was kept in the house of the astrologer, who knew how to read the time from it. He had to have an almanac next to him too. They didn't have clocks in those days. Although the British had brought clocks to India, you could only find them in the houses of the rich, and that too in Bombay, Madras or Bangalore, and the people in Malnad had merely heard tell of such an instrument.

Midnight during the month of Aashaada, and the rain fell steadily outside. The old man dozed as he tried to watch the hour-glass. As soon as all the water had trickled into the vessel it had to be turned upside down again. Everyone else in the house was asleep, except for the few old women who ran hither and thither.

'Yantanna, the head's showing', sang out Nagamma, who presided over the delivery. The old man was slightly hard of hearing. When he heard the bawling of the newborn child, he opened his eyes wide and stared at the hour-glass. What time was it? The auspicious hour of half-past-twelve had gone by. All the same, the old man wrote down the time of birth, and shouted to the women inside.

'Tippi, the child's been born at a propitious hour. I'll tell you the rest tomorrow. Can I go to bed now?'

Tippamma was Yantanna's sister. She shouted out to him:

'Yes, go to bed. No work for you now. We'll take care of the rest.'

Yantanna put away the hour-glass in an alcove and tottered off.

It was only in the morning that the inhabitants of the Anchemane heard that Sannamma had given birth. Not unusual. Some of the neighbouring women, too, came to the dark birthing room to rejoice over the baby in the dim light of a castor-oil lamp and make gestures to ward off evil spirits.

The infant girl was fair and thin. Everything proceeded as usual. On the day of the naming ceremony, Yantanna himself wrote out the horoscope: a long life, auspicious death as a married woman, a rich husband.

Every month in that house there was a wedding, an *upanayana*, a celebration of pregnancy or birth. How did one differentiate between happiness and sorrow? Once a week the cart was driven to the fair in the next village so that essential goods could be purchased for the household. Most of what they needed was grown at home. The innumerable people in the house all had work to do from morning to night. All they knew was working and eating, custom and ritual, wedding and *upanayana*.

Most importantly, they believed, like others of their century, that they should act like their forebearers did, not having the courage or the intelligence to question the right or wrong of traditions handed down to them.

Although it was more than a hundred and forty years since the British had planted their flag on Indian soil, they were still debating the backwardness and weaknesses of their subjects, and speculating as to how they could spread their influence.

Some people said the railway had come to Delhi. The postal system was introduced in Madras and Bombay, and then in the kingdom of Mysore. But it was only in 1838–39 that the post began to be delivered to every house in every village.

At that time the horse-drawn cart held sway, and helped

4

deliver the mail everywhere. Horse-carts were arranged at intervals of twenty-five to thirty miles, with horse, postman and guard taking their rest at the village where they emptied the last mailbag. Another horse-cart would be provided here. The mailbag was bound by a chain and had a lock and seal on it. When it reached a district or a taluk the local postmaster used his key to open the lock and sort the letters for the different villages. Twice a week the post came, and the delivery men were supposed to be present on those days. Each man had to take the post to about twenty-five or thirty villages, on foot. They were given footwear, khaki pants, a coat, and khaki headgear by the government. And a thick staff of black wood with a brass ring at the tip, with twenty or so brass leaves threaded through it. What an event it was when the postman set off in his uniform, with the mailbag on his shoulder, holding the staff sideways and jingling the brass leaves! The British had christened him a 'runner'. After leaving the post office, the runner had to stop first at the house of the lord of the taluk, the *mamaledar* or the *amaldar*, to deliver any mail they may have received. In four days, the runner had to cover at least twenty villages, only if they had any letters, of course. But the pay was not to be sneezed at. Two rupees a month! It was like two thousand then.

Besides, most people were illiterate. Only those who had passed the A and B class by scrawling the Kannada alphabet on the sand in the temple could obtain the post of runner. All other learning was in Sanskrit, passed on by word of mouth. Hardly anyone except the Brahmins took their lower secondary degree, and the post of *amaldar or sheikdar* was theirs alone, for all the others could only affix their thumb impressions.

When the runner came to a village shaking his staff, the entire population surrounded him to hear the latest news. On the verandah of the Shanbhag's house it was announced who had a letter that day. The card was read aloud by the Shanbhag, or by the runner. Since an envelope cost six pice and a card three, no one wasted money on the former. By some chance, if an envelope happened to be sent, it meant that it hid a great secret. Even if the recipient revealed its true contents, people discussed the 'secret' for years on end.

A sample of how an address was written in those days:

'To be delivered in person to Shanbhag Malura Krishnappa, living in the last house on the right in the street of the chariot house, in Tirthahalli, in Shimoga Taluk.'

And the card would read thus:

'Tirtharoopa Rajaman Rajashri Nanju Elder Uncle, your child Shrikanta salutes you and craves your blessings. We are all fine, let us know how you are. Everything is all right. My second daughter Rukku has had a baby son. The child and the mother are both in good health. Are you looking for a boy for our Paddi? Everything else is all right. Write us a line now and then to let us know how you are doing. My greetings to all the elders in the house. Blessings on the young ones. Have an answer written. Regards. At your command,
Shrikanta.'

One letter for a village was enough. Whatever the news was, it did not matter. That day the runner would bathe, feast and rest in the village elder's house. Before he left, he would put into the postal bag all the presents he was heaped with. In the smaller villages, the runner himself would have to read the letter out to the Gowda or Patel, since they could not read or write. The runner also carried cards and envelopes, and often wrote out an answer to the letter received. The lord of the house would say respectfully, 'Write the reply yourself, Sir. You can put down everything as usual and then I'll say a few words.'

The postman also provided writing implements: an ink-pot that wouldn't spill and a swan-quill. He mixed a pinch of ink powder in a little bowl, wrote out the message on the card and read it out to the assembled household. After this, he would be fed with milk, bananas and jackfruit. The Gowda would place a pile of homegrown foodstuff in front of the runner and make his request: 'Sir, lord, you must take this letter yourself to our relative and bring back a reply.'

'Certainly,' the postman would say, struggling to carry his presents. If the load was too heavy, he would be loaned an ox-cart.

In such times was Phaniyamma born in the Anchemane, the Postal House of Hebbalige.

Two

In those days, a girl's childhood, especially in a village, was circumscribed, untouched by the larger world. Phaniyamma's infancy and childhood passed in a kind of innocence. The Brahmin lord's temple school was only for the boys, and the girls never learned to read. Since the house was full of grandmothers, younger aunts, elder aunts, mothers-in-law, it functioned as a training centre for the little girls. Housework, cooking, cleaning, singing, washing the god's prayerthings, swabbing floors and sketching *rangoli*—these girls learned when they were barely two years old, as also the concept of *madi* purity. There were always of course the hundreds of festival days, and the weddings and *upanayanas*.

Although Hebbalige was a small village, since Tammayya's family was part of the postal service they delivered invitations to all the neighbouring villages when a ceremony was performed in their house. Not a day did Tammayya spend around the house, for he had to scurry like a dog to the other villages; but there was the pride of being a Government Servant, and earning two rupees a month.

By and by all the surrounding Malnad villages fell into Tammayya's bag. Not one man but four shared the work now. The salary amounted to eight rupees; with the fringe benefits, the home they owned, and their fields and crops, the Anchemane household became a name to be reckoned with in the region.

In those days when there was no newspaper, the arrival of a man from the Anchemane would bring out even the toddlers of the village. The runner not only brought letters,

8

he also carried news far and wide, retailing gossip and rumour with skill and relish. Tales of hatred and jealousy over trifles; people practising black magic on one another; taking the name of the Mother of Gajanur and the God of Dharmasthala to make a petty point; the Panchayat meetings beneath trees to resolve disputes in the presence of a big landowner—the postman told these and other stories.

On this side were the villages of Malur, Hiresave, Guddadamatha, Sheeke, Konandur, Madur, Guddepalu, Baalagaaru, Bhandya, Kukke, Kasagaru, Kallahalli, Heddur, Agaramegaravalli, Bhimanakatte, Virupakshi, Devangi, Kuppalli, Ambuthirthanagara, Chandanamakki.

On the other side were Simbavi, Situr, Lakkunda, Kauledurga, Kallur, Konaru, Halemane, Hoovalli.

Close by were Aklapur, Devalapur, Somalapur, Haalamattur, Hosa Agrahara, Thirthamattur, Ullatthi, Kithandur, Nijagur.

Beyond the stream at Thirthahalli lay Kuruvalli, Tenkanabailu, Melige, Nambala Lakshmipur, Gopalapur, Chibbalagudde, Andageri, Harokoppa, Dabbanagadde, Mahishi, Guddepalu.

Also to be covered by the Postal House were Mandagadde, Situr, Humacha, and Sindhaghatta. The Postal Department had given Tammayya only one uniform, so he came to Shimoga once to meet the authorities, requesting the issue of three or four sets of uniform clothes, and, on the petition of the local landowners, applied for a post office to be established at Tirthahalli. Six months later, Tammayya's efforts bore fruit. A post office came to Tirthahalli. So did a postmaster.

In those days when there were no petrol-driven vehicles the postal bag travelled in a horse-cart from Shimoga, with a change of carts at Mandagadde. Horse and driver rested there until the following day. Soon the driver began to take along a few passengers to provide help, courage, and company. There was another change of carts at Malur, then straight on to Tirthahalli. Slowly the number of passengers in

9

the postal cart increased. One anna up to Mandagadde, two annas to Malur, four to Tirthahalli. Since the Postal Department horses moved very fast, it was possible to leave Shimoga in the morning and reach Tirthahalli by four in the evening. And one would get off anywhere one wanted to. To those who used to travel three or four days by foot, carrying little children and provisions and luggage, Anchetammayya's arrangement came as a boon.

Two pairs of new uniform clothes were provided to Anchetammayya's establishment. Two pairs of footwear, and two brass-leaved staffs. The uniform was too tight for Tammayya, and too loose for his younger brother. But it was after all a Government Job, with two rupees a month as a salary. And the connections with all the rich men of the villages under the jurisdiction of the Postal House.

The wealth, prestige and power of the Anchemane grew greatly, but what did not change, except perhaps to increase a little, was its people's adherence to the traditions, the *madi* beliefs and the superstitions passed on to them over the generations. They believed strongly that whatever they did was right. And no one countered them, since they were all frogs in the same well. As for the women, they did not know the world outside. Their entire life was spent in the kitchen, always cleaning, cooking, preparing for weddings, pregnancies, births, shaving their heads as soon as their husbands died. If by some chance a young widow became pregnant, the ensuing uproar would end in her excommunication by the Mutt at Sringeri. After which she would be treated as the property of the entire village, forced to work in every household to earn a bite to eat, her children to belong to the caste of the untouchables.

Anchetammayya's grandfather was adept at preparing horoscopes, at telling the future from cowrie shells, at casting spells and handing out talismans. By luck or by skill he managed to cure several diseases. Besides, he knew a little bit about local medicines. In those days, people hadn't heard of hospitals and doctors and midwives. Every grandmother knew what to do when a person fell sick. Somehow people got cured, through herbs and spells. Those whose time had come, died. Those who were strong managed to survive.

In those days diseases were not called by their English names. If someone died of a heart-attack, people would praise his fortunate death: 'Lucky man! Died where he sat. Didn't suffer one bit.' No one knew what blood pressure could do. They would say that they felt giddy, or tired. Typhoid was called *sanni*, diphtheria *lalasankole*. There were no injections, but there was medicine all right. Very few people died in middle age; most lived to be a hundred or more. Perhaps it was the even pace of life, constant hard work, good food, air and discipline.

No one knew what it meant for a woman to have a difficult birth, or not to have milk for her baby. Perhaps one in a thousand died in childbirth. People in those days could face any difficulty. They had a great deal of strength, courage and patience.

Sometimes the cattle would fall sick. They too were given medicine by those who owned them. When the plants or trees—arecanut, coconut, the crops—were struck by disease, they were tended by the people of the house. It wasn't difficult. They didn't complain, because they didn't know whether happier lives than theirs existed in the world.

A few years after the Post came, the money order system was introduced, causing astonishment and confusion in its wake.

So in the Postal House, amidst hundreds of people our heroine Phaniyamma grew up quietly in the bonds of tradition. Among the twenty-odd girls in the household, Phaniyamma was the shortest. She was of small build; her complexion pale, like the *kedage* flower; her eyes small, like her nose and her mouth. She was always very gentle. Walked softly like a cat. Worked without any fuss. Spoke softly and slowly.

Everyone woke at dawn in the Anchemane. The women and girls began work at once. The men went off to work in

11

the fields or to distribute the mail. The old men bathed and began their puja and other rituals. Some women milked the cows and churned the buttermilk. The boys and girls too had plenty of work to do. The girls had to swab the doorstep and the *tulsikatte* before decorating them with *rangoli*; they picked heaps and heaps of flowers and made chains with them; they went to the pond in the garden and washed clothes. From very early in the morning the old women went about their tasks reciting the Ramayana, the Mahabharatha and various *slokas* that all the children learned by heart. The boys of the house sat in the courtyard, leaning against the pillars, reciting these poems loudly for Grandfather to hear. Grandfather spoke the Ramayana every day in front of the gods, so everyone in the house knew the verses. Besides, during the harvest there would be little plays as well.

The men boiled and dried the arecanut while the entire household joined the servants in wielding the *mettukatthi* to take the rough skin off. The peeling process went on until one at night, and then everyone slept. To entertain them while they worked, they had the amateur players from the village who put on performances during the harvest season. They had plays even at weddings and *upanayanas*, mostly from the Mahabharatha: the fight of Babruvahana, Srikrishnaparijata, the battle of Rama and Anjaneya, and others. There were no sound-boxes and harmoniums at the time, so the only instruments used were the *ekanada*, cymbals, the flute and the *mrdanga*. No make-up, no costumes. The players sat in a circle in the middle of the vast courtyard. They were all men, and they played Draupadi, Kunti and other women characters too. They did not tire of repeating themselves, and their audience did not mind hearing the stories over and over again. The players recited the verses with great vigour and ended by banging on the drum. The entire household listened while they peeled the arecanut.

Sometimes a reciter of the *harikathe* would show up, and tell his stories until the harvest ended. He would be fed well every day, and then sent away with as much jaggery, rice,

arecanut, and banana leaves as he could carry. Occasion
when a troupe of *bhagavatas* came to the village, people wou
come from all over to listen to them, and enjoy the
hospitality of the Postal House.

There was always plenty of rice, jaggery, milk and curd
and vegetables. The women cooked and served, and the
visitors ate their fill and burped. The drink called coffee was
unknown in those days, being put in the category of
untouchable especially by Brahmin households. The children
drank milk, the old men a brew of ginger and pepper. Guests
could chew as much betelnut as they wished. Or else there
was snuff. Although the missionaries were active all over the
kingdom of Mysore in those days, they had not yet reached
the Malnad. People had heard of the coffee bean but had not
yet seen such a thing.

In this atmosphere, like a plant of jasmine, Phaniyamma
grew quietly. She did not say very much, and spoke only
when she was spoken to. If her friends pressed her, she would
play cowrie games, or *gujjuga* or *channemane* in her spare time.

In those days boys wore the sacred thread at the age of five
and girls were married off between seven and nine. Ten years
was considered too old for a girl. Soon the search for a groom
for Phaniyamma began.

Three

Since Tammayya went constantly from one village to another, there was no problem about finding a bridegroom. One day he came home with a dozen horoscopes. All the boys were from families they knew; Phaniyamma's own grandfather checked the horoscopes, for his word was treated as final.

At that time no one asked the bride or the groom whether they agreed to the wedding. To see one another would of course be a major sin. The elders of the house, that is, the bride's father or grandfather would go to see the boy. They didn't demand that he have any schooling; it was enough if he knew the *mantras* for *sandhyavandane* and the prayers to the gods. If the boy came from a priestly family, he was expected to know how to conduct all the rituals. Apart from this, good health and a sound constitution were the only qualifications required.

In those days, men wore their hair in a little ponytail. Their daily attire consisted of a short dhoti and a cloth over their shoulder. Only when they had to go to the Yellamavasye festival at Tirthahalli, or on a pilgrimage to Udupi, or to celebrate Navaratri at Shringeri, did they put on a fullsleeved shirt fastened with strings, and tie on a *kachche* dhoti and a red cloth around their heads.

One long-sleeved shirt was known to be handed down over four generations. It was the same with the women. When the bangle-seller came to the village, every woman and girl bought bangles. At that time there was only one kind of bangle, with a black stripe on it. The bangle-seller would

14

cover the women's arms with bangles and leave some extra ones behind. He wasn't paid in money; instead, he was given grain and jaggery and arecanut. During Ugadi, Deepavali and Gaurihabba, the bangle-sellers had to travel to all the villages in the region in order to make a living.

As for children's clothes, when the men went to a nearby town on business, they would have something stitched for them. When the little girls were eight years old, they were draped in an eighteen-yard sari, with the pleats forming a banana-clump as large as a pillow in front, and with a silver girdle around the waist. On the knife-board used for chopping vegetables, the old women would cut the nine pieces of cloth needed for a blouse, and the girls would sew them any which way. Only in the rich people's houses could you see Dharmavaram, Kanchi and Kumbhakona silk saris in those days. In a middle-class home you saw the *kuthaala* sari, and that too only on special occasions.

It was already a year since Phaniyamma had started wearing a sari—it was imperative that she get married soon.

The horoscope of Nanjunda, the fifteen-year-old son of Melige Nilakantha Bhatta, seemed to match Phaniyamma's. The boy's fortune included a long life, a happy marriage, good stars, a good clan name. Tammayya went to Melige to convey the glad news to Nilakantha Bhatta. Both households agreed to the wedding. No need to ask the bride and groom, of course. Besides, they were children, and their elders did everything for their good, didn't they?

Nilakantha Bhatta was proud to have the Anchemane offering his son a bride. It would be useful too, to be the in-laws of the Postal House.

Perhaps Phaniyamma had seen Nanjunda from a distance at some wedding feast or the other, and that too about four years ago. She didn't remember a thing about him, of course. It didn't occur to her to say, like today's young women might, that she didn't want to get married.

So the wedding got underway. A veritable factory of *happala* and *sandige*, heaps of sweets and savouries. Tammayya

15

had gone in person to distribute invitations in all the villages that came under the Postal House. They were not printed like they are today, but written out carefully by hand. Everyone loved to attend an Anchemane wedding. Fifteen days before the event, people started pouring in from the villages. Four covered carts, each drawn by two oxen, were sent off to fetch the bridegroom's family. All the Brahmin households in Hebbalige were filled with Tammayya's relatives. Each wedding in the Anchemane took place in this fashion, and there was at least one wedding a year. The ceremony would last eight days. In those days one didn't finish the rites in half a day.

Around forty priests had gathered in the Anchemane. The bride had learned the songs she was supposed to. The sweets had been prepared.

For those eight days no one in Hebbalige lit their kitchen fires, since everyone ate at the Anchemane. The two children the bride and the groom—sat in front of the sacred fire twice a day, their eyes swollen with the smoke. No one paid any attention to them. All was as usual.

Since the bride was supposed to be shy, Phaniyamma hid her head between her knees and sat bent over on the wooden seat. And the bridegroom? He merely stood and sat, sat and stood as the priests directed him to.

No one wore suits then. However rich the bride's family was, all they would give their son-in-law was a copper plate, a vessel made of the five metals, *sankalke panje*, a turban, a stick for the pilgrimage to Kashi, an umbrella, and a pair of slippers.

Twice a day some relative had to help the fifteen-year-old Nanjunda wear his eight-yard *panche* in the right way, and tie it firmly with a string round his waist so that it wouldn't slip off. His little head was adorned with a large turban, and a jewelled *basinga*, a headband as large as the crown of the Lord Venkateswara in the great temple at Tirupati. Little Phaniyamma had to wear an eighteen-yard Puttana Paitne sari, and more jewellery than she could carry. By the end of day, Phaniyamma was sore with the burden of her ornaments.

Tammayya's family had one set of jewels which had been handed down as heirlooms. When a girl was given in marriage, all she got was a pair of gold earrings and the *mangalsutra*, but for the next eight days she had to wear all the jewellery owned by the Postal House. This was the tradition; this was what was considered appropriate for such an occasion.

Since the jewels were heirlooms they weren't given away to any of the women. Besides, the Anchemane was an undivided household. On feast-days, the eldest grandfather would remove the key from his sacred thread and take the jewels out of the trunk to hand out to the women. One got the necklace of moonlike gold beads, another the flat gold one, yet another the flowery gold ornaments for the hair, or the clasps with the image of a cobra. As soon as the festival was over, the jewels had to be returned to Grandfather. It was only when a girl got married that she wore all the jewels they owned. These jewels were often loaned out for other people's weddings. And sure enough, someone from the Anchemane went along to keep an eye on them.

For hours on end, the wedding songs had to be sung. Now and then the old women droned the ritual songs as well. Drowning them all was Barber Narasinga playing the *olaga*. Narasinga could play only three or four airs, and that too without much attempt to maintain any rhythm. No one paid him any attention, although his dark cheeks puffed out like a pair of bellows, the knotted veins on his forehead, and his swaying head as he played his instrument were frightening to behold. The man who sounded the drum was even more terrifying. He beat the drum as though he meant its tightly stretched skin to burst. And why not? Didn't they get two large meals a day, heaps of snacks, and finally, while leaving, ten measures of rice, arecanut, jaggery and coconut?

Tammayya's daughter's wedding was celebrated thus in the appropriate manner, with no ritual omitted. The more important in-laws were given presents of cloth; muslin shoulder-cloths for the men and blouse-pieces for the women. And the mother-in-law was given a sari. In those days, a sari cost one rupee and a blouse-piece one anna.

As was customary, the in-laws were taken back to their village in carts drawn by pairs of oxen. When they were about to leave, the bride had to bid goodbye with palms joined together, and they all blessed her. Tammayya's father swelled with pride as he described Phaniyamma's fortunate life to her parents-in-law.

'Phani's horoscope is a fine one. All the sixteen qualities came together when I matched the children's horoscopes. Lifelong bliss and the birth of eight sons is what I see ahead. I've never been proved wrong until now. Wait and see, by the time you welcome your daughter-in-law to your house, your house too will be filled with wealth and joy. No doubt about that.'

Everyone believed him. The in-laws left in a contented frame of mind. After all this, the bride had not looked at the groom. The groom had not seen the bride. Why did they need to anyway? What would they talk about? They were both children after all.

Nanjunda had not got a proper glimpse of his bride's face. He was too preoccupied with trying to get rid of his heavy clothes, the headdress, and the smoke. Everyone had to be married off. And so did he. This was as much as he knew.

The sweets and savouries he couldn't eat during the wedding ceremony he consumed during the journey back. As he munched, he asked his mother:

'Amma, are they going to do all that smoky stuff again?'

His mother laughed. What should she tell him?

'Yes, boy. They'll do it once more when she comes of age.'

'What's that, Amma?' asked Nanjunda innocently. 'Will I have to go through an eight-day ceremony then? And wear that heavy *panche*?'

Everyone in the cart began to laugh. Nanjunda grinned too, not knowing what to do. His married sister said, 'No,

Nanju, when Phani menstruates they'll perform some rites, with only one day of sitting before the fire. But after that you'll have to wear the *kacche panche* everyday.'

'So when will Phani menstruate? What does that mean?'

Again people burst out laughing.

Nanjunda's mother was on the verge of shouting at him. But she bit her tongue, and said, 'Poor thing. She's only nine years old yet. It'll probably take another three or four years.'

'Oh, that's good', said Nanjunda, relieved.

Barely two months after the wedding was the Yella-mavasye or Sesame-No-Moon-Night fair at Tirthahalli. Since it was a wedding-year the entire household, except the very old women and the servants, decided to visit the fair. Phaniyamma had seen a few of the surrounding villages, and had been once to Sringeri for the Navaratri festival, but had not gone anywhere else. And once she began to undertake fasts and suchlike, she wouldn't be able to go on journeys again.

Two cartloads of people set off to Tirthahalli. The patriarch of the Postal House brought along the cashbox and the jewellery. Since several carts had set out from the neighbouring villages, they all met on the road to Tirthahalli, all twenty or so of them.

By the chariot shed of Tirthahalli lived Tammayya's relative, Venkataramanayya, at whose house they were to stay. At fair time, people's houses were filled with relatives from all over.

All along the street, on the rocks, camped the families of the shopkeepers who had brought goods to the fair. They slept around their stalls to safeguard their wares. Since in those days there were no streetlights, the merchants them-selves used to bring brands and lanterns, and take turns keeping watch. Often there were more theives than customers at the fair.

Four

Although Tirthahalli did not then have a police station, the rich men of the town had petitioned the Deputy Superintendent of Police at Shimoga to send a contingent of forty Special Policemen at the time of the fair. Often the police pestered the shopkeepers much more than the thieves did, demanding whatever caught their fancy at the stalls. The shopkeepers were afraid of them and their strange uniforms; so was the general public, especially the women.

Most of the stalls sold sweets, *mandakki* and roasted groundnuts. Besides there were shops for bangles, necklaces, cloth and copperware. The outdr players who put up all night performances of religious stories, the acrobats, the men with monkeys, puppeteers, palmists, actors and magicians also thronged there. Everyone had to take a dip in the Tunga river and had to get a glimpse of Lord Rameshwara. Which is why the stalls stretched from the field by the chariot garage all the way to the temple.

Tammayya's family arrived in the midst of all this confusion to stay with Venkataramanayya, whose house was next to the chariot garage. The arrival of the Postal family was a matter of great excitement for their hosts.

From the verandah of the house one could see all the entertainment performed in the street. 'Never in the last five years or so have I seen so many people as this time,' said Venkataramanayya.

On Yellamavasye, Sesame-No-Moon-Night, the last night of the month of Bhadrapada, four policemen stood by the river, tying a rope aound the pilgrims before they dunked them in the water thrice and pulled them out. The pilgrims then had to go elsewhere to finish their purificatory bath.

The legend ran thus: Parashurama, on his father Jamadagni's orders, beheaded his mother Renuka for daring to look at another sage's reflection in the water. Looking admiringly at his son's bloodstained axe, the father said he could ask for whatever boon he chose. 'My mother's beheading has purified her. I ask that she be brought back to life.' Renuka came alive and bowed before her husband. Seeing his son standing silently, Jamadagni asked him what the matter was. 'My mother has come back to life, purified. But I am tainted with the sin of matricide, a sin that may destroy all my valour. Tell me how I can absolve it.' Jamadagni looked at his son's axe encrusted with dried blood. 'Yes, my son', he said, 'your axe, dedicated to the slaying of Kshatriyas, has been contaminated by the sin of matricide. You must wash it thoroughly. Wash it once in each river in the land, and offer prayers to the god of each after you have bathed. When all the blood has been washed away, then you will be absolved. And those who bathe in that last river will find their sins too will be washed away.'

So Parashurama washed his axe in every river. Finally there was left a speck of blood, the sixe of a sesame seed. That was the day of Pushyabahula Amavasye, in the month of Pushya. On the banks of the Tunga, where the Lord Rama himself had installed an *ishwaralinga*, Parashurama was absolved of his sin after he had washed away that last drop of blood from his axe. He proclaimed that whoever bathed in the river on that Amavasye day would cleanse themselves of all their sins. Slowly the fair evolved. And on that Amavasye day the town was full of people and so was the stream. Like everyone else, Tammayya's family had a dip in the river and a glimpse of the Lord. They watched the acrobats and the bull-players who led a bull around which nodded in response to questions from the verandah. Phaniyamma had never been to such a fair. Although she would never rush forward to look at something, she watched the fun along with the other young girls.

Tammayya's old father brought out the Anchemane jewellery to distribute among the women. What fell to Phaniyamma's share was a gold clasp, shaped like the English letter 'M', for her plaited hair. That afternoon the bride had her hair neatly braided, the clasp around it, and her hair adorned with flowers. She had no earrings, but wore *bugudi, chandramuru*, and other ornaments for the upper ear. The house was filled with joy and excitement and confusion.

Until then women had never seen anything but the black-striped bangles. This time at the fair there had appeared bangles with yellow, red and white specks, causing a virtual revolution among the women. They were slightly more expensive than the regular bangles, but how beautiful they were! They adorned the wrists of most women at the fair. The Anchemane women all had new bangles from the wedding barely two months ago. But how could they not buy the speckled kind? The money had already been sanctioned by the elders. The bride, although she secretly longed for the new bangles, had not said a word.

Since afternoon they had been trying to get to a bangle-seller, but the crowds were immense. Finally around dusk the women from the Postal House were able to find some room at a bangle-seller's. By this time lighted brands had reared their heads in front of each stall.

Someone wondered aloud whether that was a good day for buying bangles, since it was a day of no moon. An old woman, lizard like, clucked, 'Where else but at a fair can you get bangles like these? And hasn't the entire town bought them all day today?'

The women went out together to the bangle-seller who was seated practically in front of the house. After dinner they were to listen to the Complete Ramayana and the recitation of the *bhagavatas* throughout the night. When Phaniyamma's turn came, she held out her wrists in silence. The lighted brand was obscured by the door of the women's room, and nothing could be seen beyond the bangle-stall. In the alcoves of Venkataramanayya's verandah glowed two little oil lamps. All around was pitch darkness. Phaniyamma felt someone leaning against her back. One of the girls, she thought. It was her uncle's daughter, Shankari.

After the bangles had been fitted onto her wrists, Phaniyamma stood up looking happily at her new acquisitions. Suddenly she felt her head was extremely light. Raising her left hand to her head, she discovered that her plait had vanished, along with the gold clasp.

In ten minutes Venkataramanayya's house had become a morass of fear, anxiety, weeping and ill omen. The bride's plait had been cut off by thieves! How could they be found in this Amavasye darkness? People believed at the time that a burglar's instrument could slice off an ear or a nose without the victim feeling it. Luckily Phaniyamma's ears were intact, although she wore many jewels on them.

There was a great deal of whispering and soft weeping in the household. Phaniyamma was put into a dark room. Her hair hadn't been very long, but she had lost more than twelve inches of it. Without any fuss, all the Anchemane jewels were returned to the patriarch and wrapped in a piece of red cloth belonging to a *madi* woman. The excitement of the past two days vanished in a twinkling. Venkataramanayya was very upset that the incident should have taken place during the Anchemane family's visit to his house. Besides, Phaniyamma's in-laws had come to stay with one of their relatives nearby. Tammayya had met them, and said that they would be leaving for their village two days hence. Now it was decided that early the following morning a cartload of people would leave, including Tammayya's old father, Phaniyamma, her mother, a coupled of old women, and several youngsters. Outside the Ramayana was being recited. The drums beat out Ravana's arrival, and the brands burned bright all round the stage. Phaniyamma looked out of the dark room, and was frightened at the sight of Ravana with his ten cardboard heads, dancing vainly in front of Sita. The drums beat louder. The ogresses around Sita shrieked and screamed.

Someone led Phaniyamma by the hand and helped her into the cart. There was no moon to tell the time by. Tammayya's father wanted to cross the town limits before sunrise. Phaniyamma lay in the middle of the cart with a piece of cloth wound tightly around her head. Those who enquired what the matter was were told: 'She has a high fever.' When they reached Hebbalige it was eight o'clock at night. Still claiming that the girl was sick, they bundled her off to a dark room. All she knew was that she had to obey her elders. Even in the dark she looked at the beautiful bangles on her wrists and was happy.

Next day the other cart returned. They tried to guard their secret. 'Phani has a fever and chill. We've got her some medicine,' they said. Theirs was a large house with people coming and going all the time. Phaniyamma must be kept in seclusion until her hair grew to a respectable length. The Anchemane family did not want the news to reach Phani's in-laws. The following month was the beginning of the winter solstice. Since it was the first year of her marriage, the girl had to perform the *puja* for the Goddess Gauri of Spring and the Gauri of Silence. She had to rush through the rites before dawn and be returned to her room before people awoke.

When Tammayya's younger brother, Chintamani, went on his rounds to deliver the mail, he stopped off to see his niece's in-laws, mainly to find out if they knew about the mishap. After dinner, as they sat chewing on betelnut, the in-laws asked, 'Is it true that you lost some jewellery at the fair in Tirthahalli? We heard someone talking about it.'

Chintamani's heart sank. He realized that this was all they knew, and tried to float a little lie.

'My third daughter, you know, a regular brat. She made a huge rumpus and insisted on wearing a jewelled clasp in her hair. In the confusion when they were buying bangles, she

24

lost the clasp. God alone knows whether it fell off or whether some thief took it. But, it's gone, all the same.'

Phaniyamma's in-laws believed him.

In a month's time, Phaniyamma's hair had grown about an inch. If the secret could be kept for another four or five months, they could actually make a braid by adding some false hair, thought the women of the Anchemane.

Within a few days, Chintamani had to go to Melige again on business. Even as he was climbing the hillock on the outskirts of Melige, an untouchable woman came up to him, weeping loudly. 'Lord, have you heard the news already?'

Chintamani stood stock still, imagining that Phani's father-in-law or his wife must have died.

'What news? I haven't heard anything. I've just arrived.'

'Nanjundayya went for his toilet by the river this morning and was bitten by a snake. He's dead!' The woman began to weep again.

Chintamani sank to the ground alone with his postal bag. The woman ran into the village to announce his arrival.

Five

Since she had to finish worshipping the *tulasi* plant and complete the prayers for the Gauri festival before daybreak, Phaniyamma had come into the yard early in the morning as usual. Although fruits were available in abundance in their house, it had become the custom in that part of the country to use only a piece of jaggery while offering prayers in front of the *tulasi*.

Phaniyamma stepped into the yard holding a wooden platter with five compartments, one of which held some jaggery. A crow which had been perched on the roof, cawing, lunged for the jaggery, and flew up in a twinkling with the food in its beak. The force of its flapping wings made Phaniyamma drop the platter, and all the turmeric and *kumkum* and ricegrains spilled on to the ground. 'Ayyappa!' shrieked Phaniyamma, once. She stood absolutely still.

Hearing her cry, Phaniyamma's grandmother, mother and aunt came rushing outside and saw what she had spilled. Without asking what had happened, her mother screamed:

'Don't you have a hold on yourself? Couldn't you have gripped the platter more tightly? One bad omen wasn't enough? Now we have the turmeric and *kumkum* spilled on a Friday morning.'

The grandmother was very fond of Phaniyamma. She scolded her daugher-in-law. 'Hold your tongue. Why don't you ask her what happened before you shout at her? Why did the platter fall, Phani?'

Phaniyamma trembled as she told them. Then she tried to scrape up the turmeric and *kumkum* from the ground. Not a pinch could she pick up. 'Let that be now', said her mother. 'Go inside and get some more so you can do the *puja*.'

'Where did this ill-omened crow come from today, I wonder', said the grandmother. 'Don't all of us perform the *puja* here every day?' She looked around to see where the crow was. It was polishing off the last of the jaggery, perched on the branch of a drumstick tree in the corner of the yard. The grandmother picked up a stone and threw it angrily. The crow flew away. All the women felt uneasy. The nine-year-old Phaniyamma did not understand a thing. She went on with the *tulasipuja*. Chintamani's wife scrubbed the yard with cowdung and erased the traces of the spilled turmeric and *kumkum*. Phaniyamma was sent back to the dark room. She was never allowed to play, but she sat in the dark and tied flowers on a string.

Two days after the incident with the crow, Chintamani came home with his burden of news. With a long face, he went and sat in a corner of the verandah. It was about four in the evening. His father was gossiping with the other old men of the village, chewing on betelnut and tobacco.

Usually when Chintamani returned from his rounds, he would go straight inside to hang up the mailbag, take off his 'unclean' runner's uniform, and have a purificatory bath. If he had not eaten, he would have his dinner before joining the men on the verandah.

Today he looked depressed, and the father wondered if one of their old relatives had passed away. Oh no, that meant ten days of mourning. At least two or three a year of these, and more than a dozen death anniversaries. 'What's the matter, Chintu?' he asked. 'Don't you want to bathe and eat?'

Chintu laid down his turban, hid his face in his hands and began to weep. All the old men rushed to his side. With the tears streaming down, Chintu said, 'Appayya, the day before yesterday morning Phani's husband Nanjunda died from the bite of a cobra. When I heard the news, I came straight back without letting even a drop of water pass my lips.'

27

In ten minutes the entire village had congregated outside Tammayya's house. Tammayya himself had gone to distribute the mail elsewhere and did not yet know what had happened. Still weeping, Chintamani told them everything he knew: 'Nanjunda had gone to his usual spot by the lake. As he crouched there, a cobra hidden in the green grass bit him between his toes. The boys who had gone to the lake with him even saw the snake going back to its anthill. It was a 'three-second snake.' By the time the pandit of Melige could bring the antidote, Nanjunda was dead. That's when I arrived in Melige. They didn't want to keep the body until people could be fetched from here, so they finished all the rites on that day. As soon as they set fire to his funeral pyre, I left for Hebbalige.'

In her dark room Phaniyamma could hear the villagefolk talking outside, and the wailing of the women of Anchemane. Her mother came in and beat her head against the wall as she wept.

'On Yellamavasye day your gold clasp went. The other day the platter fell down. I knew something bad was in store for you.'

The old women of the village comforted the mother. The usual words:

'How can anyone escape what's written on the forehead? That was her luck. Poor thing, she's a child who knows nothing yet.'

Among the women were several child-widows, who told their stories as usual. Lifelong good fortune, sixteen virtues, a long married life, the bearing of eight sons—all that her horoscope said was wiped clean and Phaniyamma was a virginal child again.

The grandfather wondered: 'I'd prepared her horoscope carefully. Did those people change the boy's horoscope by any chance?'

Not knowing what to do, not shedding a tear, Phaniyamma sat quietly. Her husband was dead. He died like everyone did. She hadn't even seen his face. While walking around the sacred fire, she had held his hand by the fingertips. She hadn't felt anything then. And now she did not weep. Seeing everyone crying, she too wiped her eyes.

The family had a great deal of work to do. The girl had not yet attained maturity. For ten days, of course, her marks of marriage would remain. And after that? This kind of problem had not been faced by any household in that province. It was seen as a problem primarily by the grandfather, the patriarch of Anchemane. All the old men who could barely hold up their trembling heads came together to say that everything must be taken care of by the tenth day. One man was prepared to go to Sringeri to find out what was to be done—every town and every family would have at least one person like this—to discover the secrets of each household and expose them patting his own back at his cleverness.

Here Tammayya himself went to Sringeri and waited two days for the decision of the Swami to be communicated to him. It was unequivocal. 'Since the girl is still a child, remove the signs of marriage on the eleventh day and have her wear a white sari. Don't touch her hair. She shouldn't show her face to anyone until she menstruates. Nor can she perform any *madi* task. The fourth day after she menstruates, her hair must be shaved off and she must be made to take up *madi* for the rest of her life. If these instructions aren't followed to the letter, the entire household will be excommunicated.'

Since Tammayya had gone from a house of mourning, which meant he was ritually polluted, he was not allowed into the *mutt*. He had sent his petition to the official in charge of the temple, and the answer only came on the third day. There was no guarantee that the petition had actually reached the Swami. People had to believe that the official's word was that of the Swami himself. Palace and temple work alike: in both you have to part with silver rupees before you get anywhere. After walking all the way to Sringeri, Tammayya had to pay fifteen silver rupees to obtain an answer. By the time he returned to Hebbalige, ten days had passed since Nanjunda's death.

On the eleventh day the old men and women of the village mercilessly broke the bangles of the nine-year-old girl. They wiped off her turmeric and *kumkum* and tore off her *mangalasutra*. Phaniyamma cried a little, only because her beautiful new bangles from the fair were destroyed.

As usual she sat in the dark room, tending some woman or the other who had just given birth. She sang in falsetto, rocking the cradle. She prepared hot treatments for the new mothers' heads. She strung flowers endlessly.

Her in-laws did not once come to Hebbalige. Some people said, 'The girl had bad luck. It swallowed the husband barely two months after their marriage.'

Much later the in-laws got wind of the incident at the fair, and the covering up done by the Anchemane. One day Phaniyamma's father-in-law's brother showed up in Hebbalige, put up at someone else's house, and came over to the Anchemane to pick a fight with Tammayya. 'Who thought the Anchemane family would cheat us like this? We would have never agreed to the marriage if we'd known about the girl. You've altered her horoscope to hide the flaws, haven't you?'

Tammayya's father was outraged. He went inside to fetch Phaniyamma's original horoscope. He flung it before the man, saying, 'Here you are, sir, this was written at Phani's birth. It wasn't created afresh for the wedding. You can show it to anyone you like. You are the ones who prepared a horoscope for a boy who wasn't going to live. I've written out thousands of horoscopes in my time, and not one had proved false. Do people pull down a rock on their own children's heads?'

Phaniyamma's in-law went away without stepping onto their verandah. All this had no effect at all on Phaniyamma. Nothing had changed for her. Now she needn't even perform the *pujas*.

Four years rolled by. One day, early in the morning, Phaniyamma began to cry. The women in the dark room were questioned. The family received the news of Phani-yamma's menstruation. All the women of the village came to visit and click their tongues in sympathy. No celebration, no *arati*, no sesame and jaggery sweets, wept Phaniyamma's mother. On the fourth day the last auspicious rite of her life awaited Phaniyamma. The women of the household sur-rounded the barber who sat under the jackfruit tree in the yard, making sure he cut off the girl's hair and shaved her head absolutely smooth.

Now Phaniyamma bent her head like a lamb and wept. Nearly fourteen now, she had grown to full stature in the darkened room. She had blossomed into youth.

No fasts and *pujas* and ceremonies for her now, unlike the other girls. She realized that until she died she would have to eat one meal a day and live with a shaven head. But what could she do? This happened to every woman whose husband died. No one had wronged her. If there was any mistake, they would be excommunicated by the temple at Sringeri.

Thus she reached the third stage in her life.

The oldest grandmother in the household gave her advice about general conduct, how to sip water before or after a ceremony, and how to pray and tell her beads. Every day after bathing, she would have to wear *madi* clothes, say prayers before the god and in front of the *tulasi*, recite the Gita and the Ramayana. Then she would have to enter the kitchen, and after that there would be no rest until midnight. The *madi* women ate after everybody else, often around three or four in the afternoon.

In the morning the children had to be provided with puffed rice, beaten rice, *hurihittu*, bread baked on coals, or even cold rice if there was nothing else. If the men had to go out to work, they had to be given something to eat after their bath and prayers. The nursing mothers had to have milk. The other women ate nothing until the midday meal. There was always a great deal of fruit around the house, and people got to eat something or the other. The only ones who got nothing were the *madi* women, the widows. But they were accus-tomed to that.

Six

Now that Phaniyamma had joined the group of *madi* women, she had to begin work at dawn: cows to be milked, buttermilk to be churned, newborn infants and their mothers bathed; and after that, *madi* clothes to be worn before prayers in front of god and *tulasi*, the several rites, meditation, recitation of the sacred texts, and then a couple of spoonfuls of the *tirtha*. Until evening there were various *madi* tasks to be carried out: chopping vegetables, pounding, grinding, scraping, straining, cleaning. What strength she must have had in that young body! Untiring, unhurried, without spilling or banging down anything, the girl did all the work she was assigned. Half-a-dozen old women supervised the task, and the girl kept asking them what she could do. Especially when summer came, there was not a second to be wasted. In anticipation of the monsoon, they had to prepare for that huge family all kinds of *happala, sandige, baalaka*, roasted nuts and pickles.

There were at least fifty people in the house for dinner on any given day. And visiting relatives besides. On feast days one couldn't even count the guests. And the weddings and *upanayanas* every year. The provisions for these had to be prepared. The beaten rice had to be pounded. The *aralu* had to be made.

In a very short time people forgot the sorrow of Phaniyamma's widowhood. She too seemed to adopt a disinterested attitude. Even if she had gone to her mother-in-law's house, she would have had to slave just the same. They didn't ask for her, and the Anchemane didn't send her. What would they do with a daughter-in-law when they had no son?

Being a widow, the girl did not drink any milk. Not a drop of milk reached her lips, although she milked the twenty-odd cows twice a day, boiled the milk, and churned the butter. She never thought about food. Around four in the evening she sat with the other *madi* women and ate a few morsels. Her next meal would be the following day at the same time. Since there were five *madi* women, they prepared a snack for themselves at suppertime. They usually had some beaten rice, *roti, dosa,* or *hurihittu,* and even the children who had long been in bed woke up to demand their share.

One of the old women would click disapprovingly:

'Look at the children these days. The've eaten fit to burst their stomachs and now they're here again for more. That's all they do—eat from morning to night.'

Some of the children's mothers did not pay any heed to this. Others were annoyed by it, and they would drag off their children and give them a couple of blows.

'You're worse than beggars, you godforsaken ones! Haven't you been eating since morning? Those people have been working all day, they eat only one meal; and when they're trying to get a bite you go and stand in front of them as if you haven't seen food in your lives! Lie down!' The mothers would fling them on the mattresses and cover them with the blankets.

The children howled for a while and then slept.

Every day there would one incident or another like this. By and by it began to bother Phaniyamma. She devised a plan, and told the children:

'Don't come to the kitchen at night for a bite. I'll bring you some food.'

As soon as Phaniyamma's share was given to her on a leaf, she slipped out and distributed it all amongst the children who were awake, putting only a small piece in her own mouth for form's sake.

The old women scolded her: 'If you give them everything,

what'll remain for you, Phani? In any case, they eat from morning to night.'

Phaniyamma did not reply. She would take her leaf to the rubbish heap in the backyard and wash her hands.

In the bloom of her youth Phaniyamma became a true *tapasvini*.

As she grew older, she began to grow in experience also. At night she would often recall all that had happened to her since her marriage. But although she was over twenty years old, she still had no idea what it mean to be male or female, why people got married, how children were born.

At first she used to sleep in the room for women who had recently delivered. After she became *madi*, she slept with the other *madi* women. Although there were more than a dozen couples in the house, in those days a woman would not be seen going near her husband during the day or speaking to him. At night, after the women had gone to bed, the men would fasten all the doors of the house before they retired to their rooms. Early in the morning, even before Phaniyamma awoke, the married women would have risen and washed their faces and applied *kumkum* to their foreheads.

Phaniyamma was about twenty-three years old when she heard the following conversation. The men were speaking outside: 'That cow Tunga isn't pregnant yet. We should have given it Nambala Nanjegowda's bull.'

Phaniyamma did not understand what this meant. So what if Tunga did not become pregnant? Weren't there lots of cows in the house which produced milk in plenty? And what did it mean to give Tunga a bull?

She was not bold enough to ask someone what the conversation signified. Besides, what business was it of hers? Quickly she forgot the incident.

Six years passed. Phaniyamma helped her own mother deliver four children. Her aunt bore a child every year. Tammayya's sisters too came here for their deliveries. It was like a factory. Tammayya's younger sister's children started calling Phaniyamma 'Atthe' and she became 'Atthe' to all the children of the house.

Momentous changes had taken place inside and outside the house. Tammayya's old mother and father had died. Tammayya himself was old now, and had handed over the mail distribution to his sons and nephews.

The old discipline did not prevail in the family. Feuds and divisiveness broke out. But no one had the courage yet to speak out in front of Tammayya.

Chintamani's daughter Subbi had been brought back to the Anchemane by her husband. 'Six years since we married, and no children. You can keep your daughter', the man had said. Two years had passed, and the man was married to someone else who had borne him a child.

'So what if she hasn't had children? Let her live alongside the other woman. It's not her fault, is it? You can look after your own wife', Chintamani had declared, taking Subbi to her husband's house.

Subbi was quarrelsome by nature. Her husband's other wife was no better. They fought every day, until Subbi's husband slapped her soundly and thrust her out: 'Go to your father's house! If you set foot here again, I'll break your leg and put it in your hand.' Subbi walked home to her village, weeping. She sat in front of her mother and cried loudly:

'That untouchable—she treats me worse than the dust beneath her feet. That man beats me like he would a cow. He says he'll break my leg if I go there again. If you send me back, I'll jump into the lake at once and end my life.'

Everyone realized matters would not mend. Subbi's mother wailed: 'This was written on my forehead. Lie here in a corner as long as I'm alive. Then you can find another home to go to.'

Subbi was a healthy, strapping woman, rough in speech and manner. The village folk held her in contempt as one who had left her husband. Phaniyamma's widowhood; the death of the elders; Subbi's rejection of her husband's home; the divisiveness in the Anchemane—all these had contributed to the decline in the Postal House's prestige. Still, Subbi bossed over the younger people in the house.

Putta Jois of Halamattur was a frequent visitor to Hebbalige ever since he had been a little boy. He attended every single festivity at the Anchemane, staying three or four days each time he came. He was a good-humoured young man with a discerning eye, and a great favourite with everyone. He told funny stories to the young ones. He had studied Sanskrit for four years at the Sringeri Mutt and displayed his learning at every possible opportunity. He was married, with two children. His wife Bhagirathi was slender and long-faced, but good-looking and a competent house-wife.

Putta Jois heard about Subbi's return from her husband's house. He said to Chintamani: 'What tomfoolery is this, sir? Shouldn't you take the girl there yourself and talk to that man?'

Chintamani said indifferently 'All that's been tried, my boy. I took her over and left her there. Then he beat her and sent her back again. I shan't go to his doorstep once more. Isn't there enough rice for an extra person in my house? It's her luck, what can we do? We got medicine for her. We had her worship the cobra. No use. We have two barren cows in our cattle-shed. But have we driven them away into the forest? They live alongside the other cows. The same with Subbi. Her husband's thrown her out, but if we do the same where will she go?'

Putta Jois raised a pinch of snuff to his nose.

'That's right. The fruit isn't burdensome to the vine. Of course she'll stay here with the others.'

Seven

Feastdays and funeral rites were excuses for Putta Jois to visit the Postal House. Although his name Putta indicated smallness, he was a tall, well-built man. The thick hair on his half-shaven head was tied into a neat knot at the back. When he washed his curly foot-length hair it hung free, black and shining. His even teeth, bright eyes and dark skin made him handsome. He amused everyone with story, riddle and proverb, and endeared himself to all with his wit and humour.

By this time Phaniyamma was about forty years old. She had not gone into menopause yet.

The big Anchemane had doors on all four sides: one leading into the street, one into the backyard, one into the garden, and another for letting out the cows and calves from their pen. Next to the garden door was the room for the women who had their periods, and this room was never vacant.

Having her period was very burdensome to Phaniyamma. She did not like sitting apart for three days every month. Not that she didn't have any work to do during that time.

It was during the waxing of the moon, and Phaniyamma had her period. That afternoon Putta Jois had come into town. Late at night when everyone was asleep, even the girl who lay in the menstruating room next door, Phaniyamma heard a slight noise outside the window, which was unlatched but open only a crack. Outside someone was whispering. Beyond the window was the room where grain was pounded, to reach which one had to go around the cattle-shed. Phaniyamma wondered who it was at that time of night. She went to the window and looked through the crack. She could hear the whispered words quite clearly, and see their silhouettes. Not knowing what was happening, Phaniyamma broke out in a sweat.

The man was saying: 'Why are you so scared, woman? Everyone's asleep. In any case you can't have children. How can you live without your husband at this age? When you're old no one will sniff around you.'

'No, Jois. I'm afraid. Phaniyamma is sleeping right here in the menstruating room. If she comes to know . . .'

'Come quietly, woman. It's two in the morning. What does your poor Phaniyamma know anyway? How is it that you're getting scared only now, after the first two days? Tell me.'

As Phaniyamma watched, Putta Jois lay Subbi down next to the grain container. 'Remove your waistband first', he said. Phaniyamma could not bear to see what happened next. She curled up softly on her mat, her limbs trembling. Mentally she invoked Shiva and Rama, but realizing that she couldn't pray while menstruating, she covered her face and head with the blanket. Still she shivered as though with a fever.

Subbi was married and had left her husband. Putta Jois was a married man. He had said that she couldn't have children. Was this how children were made? I've lived in this house forty years and not seen a sight such as this, thought Phaniyamma. I suppose all the children in our house were born like this. *Issi*, how disgusting! Marriage, menstruation, children, childbirth, family life, *Puja* and prayers, *madi* . . . All rubbish!

Suddenly Phaniyamma remembered something she had heard her father say: 'Tunga the cow hasn't gotten pregnant. Perhaps we should give her another bull.' Living as she did between kitchen and dark room, Phaniyamma had not even seen the coupling of a cow and bull.

Now she thought: 'I'm glad my husband's dead. Otherwise

the same fate would have been in store for me. Lying naked in front of a man . . . how revolting . . . *thoo!*'

From that moment Phaniyamma could not stand the sight of Putta Jois. She realised now why he came every few days to the Postal House after Subbi's return from her husband's house. During the day Subbi did not appear before Putta Jois. He spent the morning talking with and flattering the old man, Tammayya, or picking unripe mangoes for pickling and preparing dried banana leaf to be used as bowls. The women were pleased with his work.

The next night it happened again, and Phaniyamma knew she had not made a mistake. But who could she discuss her anguish with? She was herself a dependent in her mother's house. Her mother was almost entirely deaf, and Tammayya was so old that his head shook continually. Chintamani too was old. The older *madi* women were long dead. The girl Subbi, who had grown up in front of her eyes, had come to this, had she? Was the younger generation shameless? This was a sin, and why should she, Phaniyamma, sully her mouth by speaking about it? Who knows how many such incidents have taken place in the Postal House? What else will I have to witness in my remaining years, O Lord? Can't you shorten my lifespan?

The following day Phaniyamma came out of her seclusion. She observed Subbi's movements closely. The young woman shouted at the children as usual as she did her work sloppily. If her mother said anything at all, she would snap: 'I'm a homeless woman who's left her husband, and have to beg for my supper. Even you have contempt for me because I'm a barren cow. Should I go jump in the pond and kill myself?' She would begin to wail loudly. Then Phaniyamma herself would have to comfort her: 'Why do you scold her, aunt? Poor thing, she's had a rough time. At least I don't have a husband. But she has one, although she might as well not. Wasn't she born in this house? It's not good for the family if young women are made to weep.'

Although there were many cracks in the life of the Postal

House, no one ever said a word againgst Phaniyamma. This was because she tried to do what each person wanted. Even in the thick of a bitter fight, she would remain silent. Her gentle speech did not hurt a soul; she bore all burdens without complaining, and turned away from unpleasant scenes in silence. She treated everyone with love and compassion, and worked hard from morning to night, stopping only to eat a morsel or two in the afternoon. She never wanted anything. At first, she would need three coins every three or four months to pay the barber to shave her head. One of the men of the Anchemane willingly gave the money, but to Phaniyamma it seemed like an enormous expense. One day she had gone to perform her ablutions when she saw an *ummatthana* bush covered with unripe fruit. She remembered what she had heard as a very young girl. Once some of the boys had brought home a fruit from this bush to play with, and her grandmother had shouted at them: 'Don't bring that in. If a drop of its juice touches your head, you'll lose all your hair. Throw that away now.'

Now Phaniyamma wondered if the juice would really work. Then she needn't offer her head to the barber every few months and be defiled. She decided to try it.

She hesitated for a moment. Why hadn't her grandmother used the fruit then? All the same, without telling a soul, she broke open one of the *ummatthana* fruits and smeared the juice onto her head before going to bed. When she woke next morning, half her hair had fallen in clumps on her *pallu*. She threw it on the rubbish heap in the backyard. When she bathed, some more hair got washed away. On the second day, not a single hair remained on her head. But her fair scalp was swollen and red. No one noticed. There was only one other blind old *madi* woman, and she did not pay any attention. After lunch, Phaniyamma went to the provision room and prepared a paste of sandalwood. She smeared her scalp with it, put some banana leaves on top and covered her head with her sari. Some people said: 'Phaniyamma smells nice today.' She replied lightly: 'I have some boils on the head. So I've put on some sandal paste.'

For nearly six motnhs, no one noticed that her hair did not grow, and that she did not send for the barber.

Taking an old white dhoti from her father or brothers, she would make some pleats in it and knot it up as a sari. They were nine-yard dhotis. She scrubbed them clean with soapnut so that they always remained white.

Now that all the older people were dead, Phaniyamma began to be called 'Ancheyatthe'.

The oldest *madi* woman died, and Phaniyamma stopped making a snack in the evening for herself. If one of the younger married women scolded her, she would say: 'No, girls, I'd rather not cook just for myself. It's almost evening by the time I've had lunch. And I'm not hungry at night. There's all this fruit lying around; I can pop something into my mouth if I feel like it.' As a *madi* woman, she did not drink any milk. Sometimes she would eat a couple of bananas and have a glass of buttermilk at night.

One evening she had become impure for some reason or another, and didn't feel like bathing and changing her clothes just so that she could eat a piece of fruit. Why not have the fruit at lunch?, she thought. So she began to eat only once a day. In that large and divided household, no one noticed any change in Phaniyamma's routine. Even on the biggest feastday, Phaniyamma, who would prepare all the special sweets, ate a few pieces at lunchtime, and then not a drop of water until the following day.

Eight

The world had changed completely over forty years. Tammayya's household had been divided into five parts. Phaniyamma—Ancheyatthe—was the oldest surviving head of the family. Post Offices had sprung up in Tirthahalli, Sringeri, Koppa and other small towns. The Postal Department jobs had been taken away from Tammayya's family, and only the name of Anchemane remained.

The nineteenth century had passed. More than fifteen years into the new century, in 1917, the motor car appeared in Tirthahalli. The mail too began to be sent in motor vehicles. It would arrive in Tirthahalli by ten in the morning, where postmen would be waiting with their bicycles. Within half an hour, the letters would be on their way to the villages. The bicycle was one of the miracles of the British. It could negotiate even the narrowest path, and the postman on a fast bicycle was welcomed with even more enthusiasm than the runner of Tammayya's day. The postmen were sturdy young fellows who had learned from one another how to ride the bicycle. They rode the machines, chests flung out, as though they were *Pushpaks*. In the villages where they delivered mail, these postmen earned even more than the runners.

An even greater miracle was the motor car. It revolutionised travel in the Malnad region. From Tirthahalli to Shimoga was a journey of three hours. Udupi hotels had sprung up in every big town, so that people who had no real business to conduct would still make the three-hour trip to Shimoga to have a snack in the Udupi hotel and see a play. One Yellamavasye, a touring drama troupe came to

Tirthahalli. That year the town was bursting at the seams with people. They saw the gramophone, the petromax light, batteries, soda and hundreds of such wonders. Christian missionaries had by this time opened centres in the villages of the Malnad, in the southern Kannada districts and in the plains, and had converted quite a few people, especially non-Brahmins, to their faith.

Every town had its hospital, its middle school and its high school. But the ways of the people had not changed very much. In the Brahmin households in particular, the old traditions continued to be followed.

Phaniyamma's old eyes gazed on a few new things. Her uncle's son had taken over the Shanbhag's post in Tirthahalli, but one or two members of his family had remained in Hebbalige. Others were pursuing different professions in Mandagadde, Muluru, Shimoga or Tirthahalli. Phaniyamma, however, was wanted by all. She had to be present at every childbirth. When she was on such an errand to Shimoga once, she had to step into a motorised bus. Not only that, Phaniyamma was also taken forcibly by her older brother to see a play performed by the Varadacharya company at the Tirthahalli fair.

'No, brother, I won't come. Why should I go see a play and suchlike?' In spite of her protests, she was taken to see *Prahladacharitre* and *Manmathavijaya*.

Phaniyamma's brother used to berate the younger people who went to see plays, until one day someone had given him a pass for a performance and he had become a convert. He was dumbstruck at the descriptions of the Bhagavats which came alive in front of his eyes. He heard music he had never heard before, and was amazed at the lighting, the props, the acting of Varadacharya, the costumes.

The next day, he had rounded up all his cronies and praised the play to the skies. he did not miss the next play that came around. And this was the one that Phaniyamma was taken to. She did not say anything, except 'It was fine', and that too only when someone asked her how she liked the play. She did not go to watch the players again.

'I'll stay home. Why don't you all go?' she would say.

The Yellamavasye fair had changed greatly. It had become truly magnificent. It was the day that had changed Phaniyamma's entire life. No one remembered now that she had had her plait cut off on that day. But how could she forget?

Three bitter incidents had made Phaniyamma move away from worldly affairs. First, the cutting of her plait on Yellamavasye day; second, her head being shaved three days after she first menstruated; and third, the Subbi-Putta Jois incident. All this had propelled her towards a life of austerity.

In order to forget these unhappy incidents, Phaniyamma busied herself in work, and in prayer when there was no work to do. Even while she worked, the name of Rama never left her lips. No husband, no family, no bondage! But she was wanted by everyone. 'If Ancheyatthe looks after the mother after childbirth, neither mother nor baby will see a day's sickness. And the child will grow up healthy and strong,' said everyone from the Postal House and their wide circle of relatives. No one could grind the special spieces for the newly-delivered mother or bathe her as well as Phaniyamma; no one served food more gently or lovingly. Besides, having Ancheyatthe there meant minimising expenses.

By this time people drank coffee in their houses. Even the *madi* women drank jaggery-sweetened coffee by the tumbler-ful. But Phaniyamma could not stand its smell. Her wants were few. For years she had bathed in cold water. Even her one meal a day was often given a miss now. A few things happened to push her further along the road to renunciation.

Perhaps she was seventy then. The household had had lunch. It was Nagarapanchami day. Heaps of *kadubu* had been prepared and consumed. Most of the cooking and serving was done by Phaniyamma. It was five in the evening when Phaniyamma served herself on a banana leaf and sat down to eat. She always sat facing the stove. Her last meal had been the previous afternoon, and her stomach was sticking to her back. She took two sips of water, said 'Ramarama' and placed a small ball of rice and dal in her mouth. Just then a little boy came running up from behind and leaned against her, clamouring for another sweet *kadubu*. Phaniyamma turned, and saw Chintamani's daughter's two-year-old son, wearing an 'impure' shirt. Phaniyamma did not know what to do.

'Ayyo, my child, so you've touched me', she said softly. The child's mother Mahalakshmi ran up, distressed. Ancheyatthe had spent the entire day preparing the *kadubu* for forty people, and now just as she was about to eat this brat had gone and touched her! Perhaps she wouldn't eat at all now. Mahalakshmi was inordinately angry with her son. 'You worthless one', she screamed. 'You've stuffed yourself all day and now you've made your granny impure.' She dragged off her son and hit him soundly. The force of her beating made the child let out one tiny scream before he choked and vomited out all the *kadubu* he had eaten. Phaniyamma rose swiftly and washed her hands. The child was turning blue. The entire household had gathered around. Phaniyamma patted some water onto the boy's forehead and blew into his ears while she folded his arms and legs. Ten minutes later, the boy started breathing normally and opened his eyes. Ancheyatthe wiped away her tears. Darkness surrounded them. Phaniyamma said softly:

'How could you hit your own son like that, Mahalakshmi, as though he were an animal? What does a child know about *madi* and all that? What if something had happened to him?'

Mahalakshmi began to cry. She put her son on her lap and comforted him, saying, 'Phaniyakka, you work all alone from morn to night like ten servants. You only eat one meal a day. And I was upset to see even that disturbed. That's why I hit him. Please, Phaniyakka, go and bathe again and come back in *madi* clothes so that you can eat a morsel at least.'

Phaniyamma said calmly: 'What does it really mean to eat,

Mahalakshami? I've put something to my mouth and washed my hands already. Women like me mustn't eat twice, you know that. I can always get some fruit later.'

'Ayyo, and all the *kadubu* you made!' exclaimed Mahalakshmi. 'Have a bit of that at least.'

Then Phaniyamma said: 'Listen, my girls. For many days I've wanted to give up even this one meal a day. For this morsel of rice I have to struggle to keep my *madi* all day. And today my meal nearly caused the death of your child, didn't it? God has brought this to pass. Look, as long as I live I won't eat cooked food. I'm like a bamboo pole eaten by white ants. Of no use to anyone. But I won't kill myself. I'll die only after having experienced the sins of seven incarnations in this one lifetime. I don't want to be born again, but then who knows whether such a thing as the next life exists?'

The women of the household wept. They said: 'Atthe, you work so hard. How can you not eat rice at all? You may not want to live much longer, but we need you.'

She laughed: 'Foolish girls. What help do I give you? I wonder why the lord saw fit to give this bald widow such a long life. I have to pass the time, you know. That's why I keep myself busy. Do I do anything specially for you, then?'

Thus Phaniyamma in her seventieth year stopped eating her midday meal. She worked hard as usual, and when all the chores were done she ate two bananas and drank a tumbler of buttermilk, and that was that. Now she only lived to work.

Nine

It was as though the supreme one did not have a more precious dwelling-place than in Phaniyamma's heart. Although she lived on two bananas a day and bathed in cold water, the life-spirit continued to inhabit her body, of which was left only skin and bones. Her spirit seemed to carry a strange electrical charge. Not once did she complain of weariness or pain. Never in her life had she fallen ill. Her life flowed evenly like a river on level ground.

All she needed were a couple of white saris once in three or four years. Someone or the other would bring them to her without her asking. Every woman she helped recover from childbirth made sure that she was given a present of a white sari, however much she protested she didn't want it. She wore only a rag while finishing the morning chores, but after she had eaten, she changed into a proper sari and sat on a mat, rolling out *happala*, preparing *shavige*, rolling wicks for the lamps, or telling her beads. Her saris, washed with crushed soapnut berries, were whiter than the men's dhotis.

She liked best to go to Tirthahalli, Malur, Mandagadde, and of course Shimoga, because there you had the Tunga river, and she could scrub vessels till they shone, clean saris till they looked as bright as stork's feathers, and wash herself by dunking in the water as many times as she felt like.

By this time Phaniyamma was nearing eighty. Her eyesight was undiminished. Her teeth were like a row of rice-grains. Only her skin was wrinkled, and her back a little bent. But she worked as hard as ever, and her soul had achieved a state of complete detachment. Many of those who had grown up after she did had already died. She had stepped outside the boundary-line of happiness and sorrow. True, she did not have the bonds of husband, children, money, property, desire. She could not, however, free herself completely from certain kinds of social bondage.

In her forty-fifth year, she had entered menopause, so even that impurity was banished from her body. In her sixty-fifth year, she had the opportunity to make the pilgrimage to Kashi.

The British had brought the railway up to Bombay, and one could take a train to Kashi from there. After six months of debate, a group of old men and women from Malur, Mandagadde, Hebbalige, Guddepalu and other towns decided they would make the journey.

It was a major undertaking. In days past, those who went to Kashi never returned. How could one walk barefoot from the Malnad to Kashi and survive? Many would die on the way. They had to carry all their *madi* things on head, shoulder or hip and walk all day. Where they came across a river, lake or stream they put three stones together, bathed, cooked and ate. And then walked on. At night they rested at some village or town. In this way they would take a year and a half to reach Kashi. Towards the end of the journey, there were those who begged for fruit so as to have something to eat. If the pilgrims were fortunate enough to complete their prayers and rites at Kashi, they would write a letter home, which would take another year to reach their families. Several pilgrims who remembered how arduous the journey was decided to stay back in Kashi. They lived in the free rooms of the *chhatra*, and did not ever go hungry, being Brahmins. Daily they bathed in the Ganga and gained the *darshan* of Lord Ishwara. One day they would croak, and some Brahmin or the other would touch fire to their bodies in a ritual gesture and then throw the body into the river. Thus they gained salvation.

Their relatives often didn't know whether they were dead or not. And they couldn't possibly perform the last rites for someone who might still be alive. Pilgrims would usually stop at Gaya on the way to Kashi and perform the last rites for themselves, in anticipation.

In those days, one out of a thousand would return to tell the story of the pilgrimage. He would invite all the townspeople to a huge celebratory ritual, and relate his magnificent, dangerous, astounding and advenurous experiences to an awestruck crowd.

Some listened to such tales and said they did not want to undertake the pilgrimage, since they had already got the *prasada* from Lord Ishwara's temple through their kinsmen. A few rich ones would say: 'What's the use of having all this wealth if one hasn't been to Kashi?' and set off with four muscular servants to help them.

But in Phaniyamma's time the railway had come to Bombay. Those who had seen the train with their own eyes and experienced its comforts had given such enthusiastic accounts of it that their audience would go into ecstasies.

Now the Kashi trip was fun. As much puffed rice, beaten rice and *hurihittu* as they could carry they did, and uncooked rice and lentils besides. Each wielded a heavy stick. In those times there was no paper currency, or maybe only notes of large denominations. There were robbers aplenty on the road. Each man, therefore, wore torn clothes and hid ten rupees in his loincloth. The women too carried money, in the bunch of pleats which held the sari together, at the bottom of the *hurihittu* tins, in the false bottom of the pickle jar. Between sixty of them they had nearly six hundred rupees. Forty men and twenty women; of the latter only seven were married, and the rest were *madi* women, widows.

A few relatives walked the old people all the way to Shimoga before they said goodbye. Three months journey by foot took them to Bombay, where they boarded the train for Kashi. A letter to this effect reached the Malnad after four months, much to the relief of the families.

The old people were overjoyed when they saw the comforts of the railway carriage. They occupied an entire compartment, and were delighted at how much space there was to store their things and to lie down and sleep. And windows out of which they could look if they wished, and close when the didn't. Most important of all were the bathrooms. And plenty of water! The train stopped at every town. Wherever the halt was half an hour or longer, people went out to use the bathrooms.

After having spent three months to reach Bombay, they got to Kashi in three days. They were as happy as though they had actually gone to Kailash.

Kashi, Gaya, Kedar—they travelled all over the northern region. If they fell short of cash, they could always draw upon the Kashinath Sastry Society, where they could obtain money in return for a bond.

In this way, the pilgrimage to Kashi came to an end. The only casualty was a seventy-year-old woman who died of cholera. Since she had no one at home to mourn for her, the other pilgrims completed her last rites in Kashi before they left. Later they organised a huge prayer ceremony and feast. Phaniyamma had her last rites performed in Gaya, according to the old custom that provided for those who might die on the way home.

Twenty years had passed now since Phaniyamma's Kashi pilgrimage. Phaniyamma had done all that widows were supposed to do. After entering menopause, she undertook fasts and *uratas* on Mondays, on the night of no moon, on Rishipanchami, on Vaikunta Chaturdashi. She continued to eat only fruit, and to bathe in cold water. She had stopped sleeping on a proper bed when she was only nine, and used only a woven mat, an old sari rolled up for a pillow, and more old saris sewn together for a blanket. Till she fell asleep she said her prayers, and woke before anyone else, at four a.m. She would get up noiselessly and begin to do her chores.

Perhaps God wanted to test Phaniyamma's strength and maturity even at this age. When she was around eighty-two, Phaniyamma had been taken to Konandur, to a kinsman's house, to help with a childbirth. The mother and child were thriving, and Phaniyamma was getting ready to return to Tirthahalli in a fortnight.

One night it had already struck twelve. Hasalara Baira's fifteen-year-old daughter Sinki had been in labour for four days. There were no midwives in that town, except for a couple of Muslim women and a few Gowda housewives who helped out when necessary. They had all admitted defeat in Sinki's case. Sinki was a petite girl, and the child in her womb seemed full-grown. When the pain appeared to stop, the women had smeared their hands with oil and tried to pull the baby out in vain. Their hands were too big. Now they sat around the girl, weeping, having given her up for lost. At last one of the Muslim women, Jabina-bi, said to Sinki's father:

'Baira, the Sowkar's sister Phaniyamma has small hands. If you can possibly bring the lady here, the baby might live. If not both the mother and the infant will die.'

Baira wiped his eyes, and said, 'Jabina-bi, what is it that you're saying? The old woman's a Brahmin. And like a sage. How can we ask her to come here? Won't we become sinners if we do that?'

Jabina-bi went straight to the house where Phaniyamma was staying. She told the old woman what the situation was: 'Phaniyavva, your hand is small and smooth as a sweet yellow plantain. If you make up your mind to help, you can save two lives. Tell me, mother, will you come?'

Some of the older people in the house had been awakened by their conversation. The head of the family shouted at Jabina-bi: 'Don't you know what time it is? What were you doing for the last four days? Ancheyatthe has undertaken the Kashi pilgrimage, and observed the *vratas* for Rishipanchami and Nohi. Do you know what you're asking? Can you call her out to help deliver a child? Are you out of your mind?'

Jabina-bi opened her mouth to speak. Phaniyamma stopped her, saying: 'Wait, I'll be with you in a moment.'

Ten

In ten minutes Phaniyamma came out wearing a torn sari. 'Close the street door, girls', she said. 'You can open it when I come back.' Without waiting for an answer, she walked rapidly after Jabina-bi. Baira, who was waiting silently at a distance with a lantern, led the way.

Those whom Phaniyamma had left behind looked at one another. One of the daughters-in-law spoke up: 'It is like Malakka the Brahmin wanting to eat a piece of fish before dying. Why did Ancheyatthe go? After all the pilgrimages and all the rites she's performed, how can she want to go to the untouchables' area? Those stupid fools, what were they doing for four days? To come and call her out at this time of night! And for her to go just because they called her! We'll have to have a proper purification ceremony for her after this with *panchagavya* and all!'

Everyone was disapproving of Ancheyatthe for the first time. They lowered the wick in the lantern and went back to bed.

In the impenetrable darkness, Phaniyamma followed Baira's lantern into the part of town where the untouchables lived. They had laid Sinki on a mat on the verandah, having curtained off the space with a blanket. Seeing Phaniyamma, the women all stood up in fear and astonishment. Phaniyamma sat down by Sinki's side. The girl had closed her eyes, and no one could tell whether she was still alive. Baira's wife began to howl 'Phaniyavva, save my daughter somehow. Is she dead?'

Phaniyamma placed her palm on the girl's forehead. It was

warm. She beckoned to Jabina-bi, and said, 'Now tell me what to do, quickly. I've helped with hundreds of afterbirths, but I've never delivered a child before. Tell me, quick.'

Jabina put the lamp near Sinki's feet, and placed the pot of castor oil in front of Phaniyamma.

'Here', she said. 'You must smear your right hand with this oil, keep your five fingers close together, put your hand in so, and pull out the child by the head, slowly. I'll push from above. Let the blasted child die if it wants to, but Sinki must live.' She began to massage Sinki's abdomen. The other women gathered around to help Jabina-bi. Phaniyamma scolded Sinki's mother softly, 'Why are you crying so much, Yadchi? Be quiet, you hear? Can't you see everyone's trying hard?'

The woman fell silent. Phaniyamma's little hand crept into Sinki's womb and came out with the child two minutes later. A torrent of blood followed, and Phaniyamma's body went cold.

'O Lord, what filth you've created. I don't care if I've been a widow all my life. I'm grateful you've spared me this filth', thought Phaniyamma. At that moment, she thought of Putta Jois and Subbi. 'Why should one live in a human form? O Lord, if I have to be born again, give me the life of a flowering plant. I haven't committed any sin in this in-carnation. Try not to give me another life after this one.'

This was her daily prayer. People believed in those days in heaven and hell, reincarnation, punishment, and atonement. Even those who did not really believe all this pretended that they did. As these thoughts passed through Phaniyamma's head, Jabina-bi slapped the child hard because it had not yet cried. Still no sound. She turned the baby upside down and swung it briskly from side to side. Then it started to cry, softly at first. Jabina-bi gave the child to one of the Gowda women to wash. She cleaned out Sinki's womb, and more blood flowed out along with the sac. 'Water, my mother', groaned Sinki. They gave her some water. The others now bustled about. Sinki's mother joined her hands in deference

53

to Phaniyamma, and said, 'Lady, you have a hand of gold. You saved my girl . . .'

Phaniyamma scolded her again:

'Come on, Yadchi. Enough of your flattery. Look after the child and its mother first. Give me some soapnut powder and water to wash my hands, and I'll go home. I'll send tablets of musk and some linctus for Sinki if Baira comes with me. Not a soul here must breathe a word about my delivering the child, do you hear? Be careful. I'm going to say at home that Sinki had already delivered by the time I got here. Not a word, mind!' Yadchi brought hot water and soapnut powder for Phaniyamma, whose soul was revolted at the sight of all the blood. 'O Lord, what is all this?' she thought. 'This pain, this filth—do women forget it all when they go to their husbands? What a strange forgetting! How can they bear ten or fifteen children, one after the other? I don't want a human existence, and especially not a woman's.' Having scrubbed her hands thoroughly, she said, 'Look after them, girls. I'm going home. Don't forget what I said. Not a word, remember.'

'No, our lady. We won't open our mouths', the women promised.

Baira led the way as before with the lantern. Phaniyamma said to him: 'Baira, first let's go to the pond in our garden. I have to bathe before I can go home.'

'My lady, at this time of night and in this bitter cold? Baira said in a frightened voice. 'Can't you get someone at home to heat you some water?'

'Get along with you, Baira', Phaniyamma said softly. 'For nearly eighty years I've washed myself in cold water. I don't need it warmed up.'

Baira did not say another word. He stood far from the pond while Phaniyamma bathed. It was around three in the morning, and they could hear the big clock striking in the house. Phaniyamma ducked her body eight times in the water, rinsed out her mouth, said a purificatory *mantra*, and spat out water thrice.

In her torn, wet sari she reached the house and knocked on the door, having told Baira to stand at a distance. Her sister's son opened the door and asked, 'So why did they come for you? Has Sinki delivered?'

Phaniyamma stepped inside, saying, 'Tell that man Baira to wait. By the time I got there, Nanji the Gowda's wife had already delivered the child. What do I know about all that? I didn't go further than their yard, but I was still defiled. So I bathed in the pond before coming in. Now let me fetch some medicine and powders for that poor girl.'

Phaniyamma's nephew told Baira to wait, and went back to sleep. Phaniyamma gave the medicine to Baira, and shut the front door. She changed into dry clothes, but couldn't sleep. In a short while, the first cock crowed. Phaniyamma got up. By the time she had finished a few tasks, the sun came up. The women of the house had only one question to ask: 'Has Sinki given birth?'

Ancheyatthe gave them the same answer she had given her nephew. She made another trip to the pond and took some *panchagayya* on her return.

At ten o'clock Baira's wife arrived. Phaniyamma said to one of her nieces: 'Ask Yadchi if the child and mother are all right. I'm wearing *madi*. I won't come outside. Here's some cardamom medicine I've prepared. You can drop the bottle from a height into the folds of her sari. Tell her to give it to her daughter.'

The mother and child were said to be doing well. The medicine was given to Yadchi.

'Tell her not to give Sinki any rice for two days. Send them some jaggery and wheatcream so that they can make some gruel. After that it's up to them to do what they can.'

Because Phaniyamma had said so, Yadchi obtained some wheat-cream and jaggery from the rich man's house. 'I'll come again tomorrow, my lady', she said as she went away.

Phaniyamma had never once been to the birthing room in the Anchemane or elsewhere. In the dim light of oil lamps, some Gowda's wife or the old women of the house sat waiting to help. In those days childbirth was not that difficult, and women normally delivered about an hour after going into labour. Phaniyamma's sole task had been to keep ready the hot water, medicinal decoctions and pastes which the new mother would need. Now Phaniyamma had seen and helped with an actual birth. For two days, her mind was troubled. When she sat telling her beads, she would suddenly remember that those same figures had been in Sinki's womb. Wasn't that defilement? Had she become pure again merely by drinking the *panchagayya*?

She told herself what her grandmother used to say, that helping one child to be born earned one as much *punya* or merit as a pilgrimage to Kashi. But what did she need the *punya* for? In any case, a life was a life. It was precious. And saving two lives was a meritorious thing to do. One shouldn't dwell on such things, she thought, and decided to forget the whole incident.

However, as she went about her chores, she wondered about the mystery of creation. Except for the Kashi pilgrimage, Phaniyamma had hardly been outside the house, and she failed to comprehend the rules that the elders of the house had formulated.

When her own blood flowed every month, a woman was defiled. She had to sit outside the house for three days. On the fourth day, she was purified, and could then become *madi*. Many women in Phaniyamma's family continued to menstruate after the fourth day, but they were still considered *madi*. The widows who were touched by the barber were still *madi*. But those widows who had full heads of hair were considered absolutely impure even though they had never been touched by a man. Hundreds of questions about these things plagued Phaniyamma.

Eleven

Even when there were hordes of people in the house, as for example on feast days or wedding days, Phaniyamma never indulged in unnecessary talk or in fruitless debates. In every family, there were disputes about land, property, the law courts, and marriages, among others. Often these would break out into open quarrels. Phaniyamma always remained silent at these times, for she felt none of it concerned her. All she wanted to do was to serve those to whom she was indebted for her very existence.

Likewise, no one interfered with Phaniyamma's life. All she cost them was two bananas and a tumbler of buttermilk a day. Who did not want to have an Ancheyatthe who prepared, after the day's work, all those tasty things for others palates—*happala, shavige, baalaka*?

Although she kept her mouth shut and her hands busy, Phaniyamma's mind would often slip from contemplation of the Lord to thinking about the disgust of living in the world and the chains of custom and tradition. Should she leave her home and go away to Kashi and thus cast off her remaining bonds? She wondered sometimes. But who would she beg for the railway fare? She did not have a single coin to her name. As for her husband's home, it had been decided over seventy years ago that she was too unlucky to cross its threshold.

All the elders of her mother's house were long dead. Some of the younger people were also dead. An uninterrupted succession of births and deaths. Phaniyamma was a mute witness to all that had passed. She was past the stage where she rejoiced over a birth or grieved over a death.

There were many incidents which troubled and disgusted her. Putta Jois had died several years ago. Subbi was now an old woman, and a *pativrata*, a faithful husband-worshipper. Phaniyamma had never understood what *pativrata* meant, even when she heard the tales of good wives from the *Puranas* and fables. Renuka had been beheaded for looking at the reflection of the *sanyasi* who sat on the opposite bank of the river. She was turned to stone for sleeping with a god who came to her in the guise of her husband. But men who slept with a hundred women were still pure as fire.

As she thought about this, Phaniyamma recalled an incident that had taken place when she attended a wedding in Situr. It was a week after the marriage ceremony, but they were loath to let Ancheyatthe go. One day as usual, Phaniyamma had risen before dawn and made her way to the lake beyond the hillock for a bath. The bride's father, Subbaraya, had already bathed and sat on a rock changing his sacred thread. Phaniyamma stood for a moment behind a *sampige* tree, looking at him. 'Why is he changing his thread?' she wondered. Had something inauspicious happened? Then surely everyone in the house should have heard.

She waited until Subbaraya had gone back to the house, and then went down to the lake. She scrubbed her white sari hard with soapnut. Her younger relatives wanted to buy her the new soap which had come into the market by that time. She demurred at the expense, besides having her own doubts about the ingredients in the soap, which might very well be defiling.

Now she dipped herself twenty-one times in the water, wrapped the wet sari around her body, and walked back to the house, muttering a prayer to Keshava. Subbaraya was praying already, ringing the bell loudly as he did so. His wife Lacchamma was eight months pregnant.

Phaniyamma kept worrying about the man changing his sacred thread. She waited until lunchtime, and until her own meal was over. Then she said softly to Subbaraya's older

58

aunt: 'I saw Subbu changing his thread this morning. Perhaps he touched something impure.'

Parvathamma, the aunt, was a forthright woman who always spoke her mind.

'Phaniyatthe, you've been on the Kashi pilgrimage. And you've never seen sin of any kind in your life. I shouldn't be saying this in front of you, but you ought to know this. Subbu is one of those who can't keep his dhoti on. Lacchi's going to have her child in a month or so, and he still doesn't leave her alone. Now she's told him to stay away. That man doesn't bother about caste or clan. He sleeps with some Gowda woman or some untouchable at night. When he goes out, he hides a new thread in the hollow of the mango tree. If he's at the lake for a bath before dawn, I know he's been out with his begging bowl the previous night. Poor Lacchi doesn't know what to do. Her daughter's married, and she's still delivering children herself. Who can say anything to him? If someone asks why he changed his thread, he spins a tale a yard long: 'I'd gone to relieve myself over there, and stepped on a piece of old cloth. Not knowing whether it might have been an untouchable's or a menstruating woman's, I went and bathed in the river and changed my thread.' Why should it bother you or me, Phaniyamma? Each person is responsible for his own sins.'

Phaniyamma shivered. She felt sullied. She should not have said anything about Subbu. That day she could not devote all her attention to *puja* and meditation. And at night she couldn't sleep.

'What peculiar customs we have', she thought. 'If a man touches an outcaste woman, all he needs to do is to bathe and change his sacred thread, and he's pure again. If a woman even looks at another man, she's a whore. O Lord, why do you play with us like this? The left hand which washes the buttocks is used to ring the bell during your prayers. When we pray, we must join both palms to you. For every task we need the left hand. And we're not allowed to begin any auspicious ceremony with it! How many blind traditions we have! Like the banyan tree father planted that everyone hanged himself from. No one ever thinks of changing anything.'

Then she would say to herself that these things shouldn't bother her. She was at an age when she should be distancing herself from all the filth of this world.

As the days went by, Phaniyamma became even more silent. All she did was work without stopping. She went to stay with whoever wanted her to come. She tended the sick and cared for the women who had just given birth. She did not expect anything in return, did not cost very much to maintain, and refrained from interfering in others' business.

It had been many years since her uncle's son Kittappa had become Shanbhag in Tirthahalli and had gone there to live. Once when Phaniyamma had gone to Halamatthur, Kittappa had said: 'How much longer will you stay in this godforsaken place, Phani? Come to my house. Stay with me. You've spent your entire life slaving for other people. Come to Tirthahalli. You can bathe every day in the Tunga river. You can go to the Rama temple. You know you're not a burden to anyone.'

Phaniyamma did not want to hurt him, and said gently: 'Of course I'll come and visit you, Krishna. It's the same to me where I am. This barren tree will fall one day. And someone or the other will set fire to it. Anyhow, I've had all my last rites done in Gaya. They say that a sinner lives longer than anyone else. I wonder how much I've sinned. Not in this life, as far as I can tell, but perhaps in an earlier one. Ask Subbaraya whether you can take me to Tirthahalli.'

When Kittappa made his request to Subbaraya, the latter was the older man, and without waiting for his answer, Kittappa said: 'In any case you have Parvathi to help out in your house. I'll take Phani with me.'

Kittappa was a proud man, a lawyer. He believed fervently in the gods, and in ceremonial purity and impurity. Although he was Phaniyamma's elder uncle's son, he was only three months older than her. he had been the chief organiser of the Kashi expedition, and his word was law.

Whoever came to Tirthahalli had to seek the hospitality and help of the Shanbhag, so no one dared to cross Kittappa.

Thus Phaniyamma came to Tirthahalli again. She liked staying in Kittappa's house. His wife Nagamma was generous, faithful and traditional. She was fond of her relatives. Kittappa's children, Banashankari, Bangari, Savitri, and Subrahmanya were quiet children who did not speak a great deal, but enjoyed singing and feast-days. Phaniyamma was glad to be there. She looked after all the girls when they came for their confinement. Among them was this novelist, who was also bathed by Phaniyamma and given warm milk by her.

The women she cared for are still alive today. They have always been in good health. Perhaps it was her touch that brought luck and longevity, unless it was their own good fortune. Attracted by Phaniyamma's gentle ways, her impeccable work or her limited needs, all their relatives in Shimoga wanted her to stay with them. Wherever she went, Ancheyatthe wanted only her cold bath, two bananas a day, and one white sari. Now she was Ancheyatthe to everyone.

Twelve

Eight years later, Ancheyatthe came to help with the confinement of my younger aunt. I was eight years old at the time, and was living with my aunt. Although I had seen Ancheyatthe a couple of times in Tirthahalli, this time I spent nearly six months in her company, and learned a few things about her life, even if I was too young to understand the significance of some of the events. But I was not too young to become familiar with Ancheyatthe's daily routine.

Ancheyatthe in her white sari, preparing hot and tasty meals and snacks and coffee for everyone, always sitting on a low stool or mat so that her white sari would not get soiled.

The girls who were my playmates would talk amongst themselves. All the lawyers who went to the courthouse had to pass in front of their house every day. We would comment on their dhotis: 'Isn't Ancheyatthe's sari whiter than these people's clothes?'

The men would turn to look at the laughing girls in incomprehension.

Ancheyatthe would call the girls and tell them gently: 'Young girls shouldn't stand on the verandah and laugh like that. Come inside.' She did not want to hurt the children by scolding them.

When Ancheyatthe sat down after the morning's work to make *happala*, and *shavige* or to roll wicks, a crowd of children would surround her. She was an ocean of stories, although she was illiterate and had never touched a book. But she had on the tip of her tongue all the thousands of stories, riddles and proverbs she had learnt from her elders. The stories may have been absurd, but the children loved them. And Ancheyatthe knew them all—the seven-jasmined princess, the ghost tales, the *Phanchatantra* stories, the crow and sparrow tales, the story of Aladdin, and even the *Arabian Nights*. She never tired of telling these tales, and the children never tired of listening to them over and over again.

'Don't pester her. She must be tired', my aunt would scold the children. Ancheyatthe would smile: 'Didn't you do the same to me when you were a girl, Savitri? They're only children after all. Let them listen. They'll need stories to tell their children and grandchildren, won't they?'

Aunt's eyes would fill with tears and she would go inside.

'We're not going to learn Anchayatthe's patience and goodness even if we live through seven incarnations', she would say to herself.

Once or twice when my mother was in Tirthahalli during Yellamavasye, Ancheyatthe would say: 'Banashankari, this is a very holy day, my girl. I had bathed in the pool sacred to Rama and worn a golden clasp in my hair. That was the day I began my monastic existence. Whatever you say, girl, don't you feel this whole business of family and husband and children is disgusting in a way?'

'Why do you say that, Atthe?' Banashankari would ask. And slowly Phaniyamma related to her all her life experiences. Later she said: 'Many days have passed since all of these things happened. But I felt somehow defiled because my mind was full of them. You are after all a grown woman. You have a family, a husband, and children. I told you everything, so that I could feel lighter. All my younger relatives are dead. I don't know why the Lord has spared this stunted tree, but I want my mind to be pure when I go. My eyes are old. They've seen many things, but none that were pleasant. So forget what I've told you. You have a good husband, you've borne good children. I don't know why I felt like telling the blasted story of my *karma* today. I hope I won't let the words pass my lips again as long as I live. It isn't a *purana* or an exemplary tale, is it?'

When the topic of someone's horoscope came up. Phaniyamma would say softly: 'Isn't it enough to make sure the *gotra* is all right? What's the use of horoscopes? Isn't it enough if boy and girl agree to marry one another?'

On such auspicious occasions, she never spoke about her own marriage.

Once someone asked her: 'Ancheyatthe, how old are you?'

She thought about her life, and laughed: 'Ayyo, do you call a dog a grandmother just because it's old? How do I know how old I am? And what will I do with it now anyway? Am I to be married? Is it my birthday? I'm probably as old as the *arali* tree by the pond. The only one who would know my age is Kittappa, because I'm three months younger than him. I'm a tree that's never borne flower or fruit.'

Savitri's husband said: 'Atthe, you don't know what you're saying. The *honge* tree doesn't bear fruit or flower, but doesn't it provide shade to everyone who sits underneath? You are like a *honge* tree to all of us. Why do you badmouth yourself? That's like committing suicide. Our elders say that, don't they?'

Immediately, she slapped herself on both cheeks in repentance: 'Rama, Rama! That's one thing I don't want. If I wanted to do that, would I have lived so long? Even three days' fasting won't finish off this creature. Once there was an eclipse followed by *Ekadashi*. On the third day I didn't eat a bite, just to test myself. And I didn't even feel tired! Everyone in the house was starving. I cooked them a meal, and ate two bananas on the evening of the third day. It's like the Lord has put a rock where my heart should be.'

Savitri's husband wiped his eye with the tip of his shouldercloth, and laughed: 'Atthe, don't go away from this house. Stay here as long as you like. You're no trouble to anyone. On the contrary, we probably cause you a lot of trouble, don't we?'

An indescribable emotion shadowed her face momentarily. But since she never spoke in a hurtful way, she said softly: 'What does it matter to me where I am. Didn't I stay

64

six months in your house? If someone else invites me over, I'll go there and do whatever work my hands are capable of. Living a normal life is something that wasn't written on my forehead. And to ask me not to work . . . how can I not? I've never wanted anything, but for some strange reason the one desire I have is that I should die in my mother's house. My brother's children or grandchildren are likely to be in the Anchemane now. If I die there, someone or the other'll touch my body, won't they?'

Savitri's husband felt bad that he had made the usually reticent Ancheyatthe speak in this manner.

However, Phaniyamma never said of her own accord that she wanted to go, but waited for someone to fetch her.

Around this time came the news that Guddepalu Sitarama's daughter Dakshayini had lost her husband. The family also sent for Ancheyatthe.

Dakshayini had been married four years to a man in nearby Chibbalagudde. She was a strong, beautiful, and spirited woman. Within a year of her menstruation, her husband was dead of a poisonous fever.

Sitarama was Ancheyatthe's maternal uncle's grandson. Dakshayini's brother came to fetch Phaniyamma.

There was an uproar in Sitarama's house. Dakshayini had not yet had children. She was sixteen, in the full bloom of youth, and her beauty pierced the eyes of those who looked at her. Her in-laws were arch-traditionalists. The old men and women of their house insisted that the girl should become *madi* on the tenth day. Sitarama turned to Ancheyatthe in despair. Dakshayini was stubborn: 'I don't want to become *madi* now. I can't fast at night. I won't do it.' Her in-laws had sent Bhattayya to intercede on their behalf.

'What stubbornness is this, Sitaramu? She's the eldest daughter-in-law of the house besides being full-grown. Everyone's eyes are on her. If she's made *madi* and kept indoors for a year, things would become manageable. Her mother-in-law's getting old, and there are tens of people in the house to be looked after. Who's going to do all the cooking and the *madi* work? Look at your grandmother Phaniyamma. She's been like this since before I was born. Losing her husband at nine, and becoming *madi* at thirteen. We should bow to this great mother in admiration. Come, Sitarama, it won't look good if we let your daughter be.'

Sitarama looked at Phaniyamma. She was forced to speak: 'Ayyo Bhattayya', she said. 'Why do you bring up the practices of my time? I don't even remember seeing my husband's face. Sometimes I feel as though I were born this way. Times have changed so much. This is a girl who should eat well and live well. Can she bear it if you make her take on *madi* at this age?'

Bhattayya raised a pinch of snuff to his nostrils. 'Tell me, Phaniyatthe, will a tree bend when it has never been pliant as a sapling? How can we leave the girl as she is? Every single day there are feasts and celebrations in her in-laws' house. Her mother-in-law is old. They can always find people to do the work outdoors, but shouldn't there be at least one *madi* person in the kitchen?'

Thirteen

Bhattayya's inhuman attitude saddened Ancheyatthe. She who had not wept when her husband or her parents died now wiped a tear from her eye with the edge of her *pallu*. Dakshayini, who sat in the dark with her face swollen from crying, burst out: 'I won't let them do this to me. If they force me to do it, I won't go to their house. What should I do there now my husband's gone? Was I born to slave in their household? I'm staying here!'

'Bhattayya, you must think about the matter,' Phani-yamma said softly: 'The poor girl didn't live with her husband even two full years. How can you ask a full-grown girl to sit in front of the barber without clothes to cover herself properly? She has to be like me for the rest of her life. So why can't you let her be for another four years? When she's twenty you can ask her to become *madi*. You must convince her parents-in-law of this.'

Bhattayya answered Ancheyatthe cleverly: 'Phaniyamma, what should we do when you who've been like a *sanyasi* all your life speak in this way? Those people are insisting that she take *madi*. I'm caught in between.'

'Don't say that. Why should I say anything? I never even saw my husband's face. And this poor girl lived with her man for two years. Our times were different. Everything's changed now. Those who lived in the city and are old enough to have grandchildren don't even feel the need to shave their heads. So what if a woman has hair on her head? Does all the impurity rest there? What punishment do you want for a child who has just begun to open her eyes? I'm deeply grieved by this, that's all.'

In all this time no one had ever objected to anything Phaniyamma had said. Now Bhattayya sat stubbornly in front of her. 'Oho! You've learnt many citified ways of late, Phaniyamma. You've climbed the bus and the train and seen plays and lived in the town. But a woman like you shouldn't be saying what you're saying.'

Phaniyamma rose quickly to her feet. 'You're younger than I am, Bhattayya. You needn't worry about me. There's Sitaramu and his wife and their daughter. Talk to them. I was sad that my kind of life should be inflicted on a young girl, and I said a few words because you asked me to yourself. I'm only awaiting death. Why should I meddle in this? I leave you to your fates.'

She went inside. Bhattayya felt humiliated, but did not show it. Phaniyamma sat on the back porch, her eyes shut.

Dakshayini forgot that she was in mourning and therefore impure. She ran to Ancheyatthe and hugged her, wailing: 'Atthe, I won't shave my hair off. I can't live like you! Please help me. Don't let them do this to me.'

Phaniyamma stroked Dakshayini's head, her eyes still shut. Her eyes had dried up. Her mind felt like a clear crystal.

Then Dakshayini's mother Gauramma ran up and pulled her daughter away. 'Ayyo, you inauspicious one! Why did you touch Ancheyatthe?' She hit her own head again and again and wailed.

Phaniyamma scolded her. 'Be quiet, Gauri. So what if she touches me? It's like beating someone who's fallen from the attic with a rod. Aren't you her mother? Has your heart turned to stone?'

The mother wept loudly. Dakshayini said fierily, 'Let's see them do it.'

Neither Phaniyamma nor Gauramma understood what the girl meant. She sat as still as a rock. On the ninth day she removed her mangalsutra, wiped off her *arashina* and *kumkum*, and waited in a dark room. Bhattayya had proclaimed to everyone that Dakshayini was refusing to take *madi*. Twenty-odd *madi* women from the town had come to speak to her. Although Dakshayini was known to be tough, the old women wanted it to seem as though they were doing something wonderful by talking to her.

They spoke about heaven and hell, sin, *punya*, reincarnation, etc. Dakshayini was like a madwoman. Ancheyatthe had gone into the garden to be by herself. Gauramma sat weeping in a corner. Dakshayini stood up in the darkness and roared: 'Tomorrow morning I'm going to have my head shaved. You can all come to an *arati* for me and get your coconuts and betel leaves. Are you satisfied now?'

The women stood up too, alarmed. Wondering if the girl had gone mad, they walked out, saying one by one: 'Let her do what she likes. What business is it of ours? Let her go to hell.'

Before dawn the next day Dakshayini's head had been shaved. She did not weep, did not struggle. Ancheyatthe was not to be found. Everyone searched for her high and low, in the garden, the fields, by the lake. Sitaramu knew that she was deeply hurt by what they had done to Dakshayini. That evening, after dark, Ancheyatthe returned.

No one dared ask her where she had been all day. The house was silent as a cremation ground. Dakshayini sat in the prayer-room, wearing a red sari, her head covered. Ancheyatthe sat by the *tulasi* plant in the dark. Gauramma went to sit by her, crying: 'It's all over, Atthe. You've had to bear this all your life. Why have you not eaten anything since morning? Come, have a bath and eat some fruit. After all, it was written on her forehead.'

Ancheyatthe said calmly: 'I don't want anything to eat today, Gauri. Don't put pressure on me. It won't hurt to fast for once. It is a strong soul I have. Go and comfort the girl, and make her a snack, since she can't have a meal.'

Gauramma knew it was no use begging Phaniyamma to eat something.

In Dakshayini's husband's house the last rites had begun.

Ancheyatthe got a boy to accompany her, and walked to Kuruvavalli, from where she crossed the river by boat, and came to Tirthahalli. She was now tired of living. She told Kittappa all that had happened, only to have him say: 'Let them destroy themselves. What is it to you? Why don't you stay here quietly?'

In the next two years, the sequel to Dakshayini's story spread through all the villages of the Malnad and finally reached Tirthahalli. The man who brought the news was none other than Bhattayya.

Dakshayini had become pregnant by her brother-in-law, and given birth to a baby son without going to her mother's house. Her in-laws had tried to drive her home when they learned that she was pregnant, but she had not budged. She stood up to her own mother-in-law: 'It's your son who's filled my womb. Why should I go to my mother's house? *You* can take care of me when the child is born. One son instead of another, what's the difference?'

'We'll have you excommunicated', said some old men, tying up their dhotis and setting out for Sringeri. She was unmoved.

'I'll go with you', she said. 'I'll tell the Swami all that you did. I'll see how he can excommunicate me. If he does, then I'll drive you all from the house and live here by myself. What will you do to me? If you try anything, I'll bring untouchables into the house.'

She must be mad! Or maybe she is possessed by a malevolent spirit. The men who had set out for Sringeri stayed back. Dakshayini grew her hair again. Once when the barber had been asked to come, she pushed her mother-in-law into the yard and told the barber to shave the old woman's head instead. The barber, who knew Dakshayini's history, took up his instruments and ran for his life.

No one came forward to offer their daughter in marriage to Dakshayini's brother-in-law; if there was a funeral, no Brahmins came to the house to partake of the last feast; no festivals and holy days were celebrated. If they got a medicine man to drive the spirits from her, Dakshayini would threaten them with broom and slippers. The mother-in-law helped her during childbirth without saying a word. The baby was a lovely one. But the household's *madi* practices had been thrown on the rubbish-heap. Although this story had been passed on by word of mouth and come as far as Tirthahalli and Shimoga, Kittappa's household had not heard the details until Bhattayya related them over the midday meal. Bhattayya hoped that the forthright Kittappa who respected *madi* would suggest a solution or at least condemn Dakshayini's behaviour. Instead, Kittappa said as he ate his rice and buttermilk, 'Good for her. Thank god she went with her own brother-in-law and not with an outsider. Are those people cattle, or donkeys? What was the big rush to shave the head of a sixteen-year-old? She hadn't had a chance to live happily, to have children. At least she could have been left alone in her mother's house for some years. In these days even old women don't take on *madi*. The girl did the right thing. The child's of their own house, isn't it? It'll inherit the property. Nothing wrong in that.'

Bhattayya felt humiliated. Phaniyamma, who was serving them, did not open her mouth. Bhattayya could not remain silent. 'That's all very well, Kittappa. And why did your family make Phaniyamma take on *madi* at thirteen? Why didn't you oppose it then?'

'Oho! You want to get at the root, do you? Listen to me. There's only three months' difference in age between Phani and me. Besides, she lived in Hebbalige and I in Heeretota. You want to know about something that happened eighty years ago. If things are like this now, don't you think they were much worse then? You'll see, things will change even more in the future.'

Realising there was no point arguing with Kittappa, Bhattayya got up and went to wash his hands.

Fourteen

When I went to Shimoga after my marriage I saw that Phaniyamma, who was visiting her brother's grandson's house, was thin and shrunken. She had always been slightly built. And now age, constant hard work, the death and the pain of the lives around her had crushed her. Even now her relatives did not stop bothering her.

'Ancheyatthe, it's been a long time since we tasted your tamarind *saaru*', someone would say. 'I'll make some for you tonight. That's not a problem', Phaniyamma would reply. Another person would want to eat the *patrade* she made, or her *togarinucchinunde*, or her *kadubu*, or *shaavige*. She prepared all these delicacies and served them, even though she never tasted a single thing.

'Phani's palm has the line of Nala', Kittappa used to say. 'That's why her cooking is so delicious.'

Neither praise nor condemnation affected Phaniyamma. If she heard excessive praise, she would usually slip quietly out of the room.

Kittappa's daughters were expert embroiderers and singers. Phaniyamma had helped them all with their confinements. The women had great respect for Phaniyatthe, especially since they had heard about her sorrowful life.

Ancheyatthe loved to listen to the women singing. She asked them to sing all the hymns of Purandara and Kanakadasa. She was also fond of the children's songs. As she sat rolling wicks, she would say: 'Come, child, sing 'Krishna, I won't guard any old door' for me, there's a good child.'

This time when Phaniyamma was in Tirthahalli, the

wedding of Banashankari's eldest daughter Sarasi was being arranged. 'The horoscopes match perfectly', Banashankari said. 'We wanted this boy for our daughter. He's studying. Handsome, besides.'

Ancheyatthe had seen the boy. She said softly to Banashankari: 'You mustn't rely too much on the horoscopes. Just check the clan, that's enough. My father looked at my horoscope and went on and on about my eternal wifehood. You see what's happened to me. It's enough if the boy's healthy and good-looking. Just go ahead with the wedding. Don't show the horoscope to twenty-odd people.'

Phaniyamma's words had a hidden meaning. If ten people read the horoscope, they would predict ten different futures. Which one was to be believed? She had seen hundreds of weddings, and now had attained a state of complete renunciation. Now and then she would say to Banashankari: 'I am like the waterdrop on the *kesuvu* leaf.'

For some reason she was very close to Banashankari. While rolling wicks or making *shaavige* in the afternoon, Phaniyamma would tell the younger woman all the details of her past, softly, almost under her breath, and only if there was no one else around. If she saw anyone, the only words to escape her lips were, 'Rama, Rama.'

Sometimes she would say: 'My father died giving advice from the Ramayana. All the *Puranas* and fables fill my head and my mouth, Banashankari. It's just a hobby, it seems to me. What kind of happiness did the great mother Sita experience, having wedded the Lord Rama himself? A life of trouble she had. And did her husband give her joy? He made her jump in the fire, and sent off a pregnant woman to the forest. And Draupadi, did she not suffer? Doesn't she say: 'With Arjuna for a father, Indra for a godfather, and the Lord Krishna for an uncle, why did my son Abhimanyu die? Why did the Pandavas suffer so much if Krishna was on their side? Some good-for-nothings write the *Puranas*, and we useless ones believe them. That's all there is to that.'

Ancheyatthe did not speak these words in front of anyone

else except Banashankari, who she knew would not repeat them. The other sister Savitri was an inveterate gossip. Everyone knew that to tell her anything was to kiss the mouth of the conch-shell.

By this time Banashankari's mother had died, and the nursing of Bangaramma after she had given birth to a child fell to the lot of Ancheyatthe. It was the month of Shravana. The Tunga was full and flowing fast. One day as usual Ancheyatthe set out for the river very early in the morning with a white sari folded under her arm. The sky was full of rainclouds. The rain came down in a drizzle. Since the river was full, it washed the feet of the *arali* tree. Acheyatthe sat down on a rock at the base of the tree, and saw a boat approaching through the rushing currents. Although it was still dark and raining besides, Ancheyatthe's eyesight was sharp. She could see it was a boat from Kuruvalli, and seated in it was the white-clad Premabai. 'She must be coming back from delivering a child,' thought Phaniyamma. The two boatmen tried their hardest to keep the boat on course, but the current kept turning it around.

Premabai was a young, unmarried Mangalore Christian girl of sixteen. It had only been a year since she came to work in Tirthahalli as midwife. At first the women hesitated to call her in to help. But she had won people's hearts with her smiling face and kind words. Her older sisters Sophia and Sumitra taught in the primary and middle sections of the girls' school in Tirthahalli.

Premabai too recognised Ancheyatthe. By the time the boat reached the *arali* tree, the girl was completely soaked. She looked agitated. As she disembarked, the boatmen said: 'Go and get the doctor right away, lady. How long do you want us to suffer in this rain and cold?' They sat shivering under the tree. It was at least three furlongs to the hospital and to the doctor's house. Phaniyamma asked: 'Why, girl, did someone give birth? Why do you need the doctor? What's happened?'

Premabai broke into tears. The doctor was an old man,

74

given to fits of temper. On the slightest pretext he would lash out at the patients, the nurses, and the servants. Prema said, weeping: 'Phaniyamma, it's Tippa Jois' third daughter-in-law. She's been in labour for three days. They sent for me yesterday evening. When I get there, I see that the child is stuck sideways, and the umbilical cord is around its body. Puttamma's shrieking is unbearable. I didn't sleep the whole night. The child hasn't moved one bit. Now there's no other alternative but to remove the child with forceps. If I tell the doctor he's going to start shouting at me. I don't know what to do. Why did I ever become a midwife? My sisters have such comfortable jobs, but look at me!'

Phaniyamma was silent for a second. Then she said: 'Come on, girl. I'll make a *mantra* and Putti will deliver the child soon. Let's go.'

Premabai's eyes widened. 'Really, Phaniyamma? Will she deliver safely? I'll fall at your feet if that happens.'

The boatmen and the two women got into the boat. The current was strong enough to strike fear into the hearts of the passengers. But the boatmen, as though inspired, took them to Tippa Jois' house on the other bank in fifteen minutes. A group of *madi* women as well as others had gathered there. Everyone stood up at the sight of Phaniyamma, who did not allow anyone to speak, but said straightaway to the girl's mother-in-law, 'Achchamma, get me a lemon, a knife, a turmeric root, and a bit of coal. I'm going to say a *mantra*. In ten minutes Putti will give birth.' Everything was brought. Phaniyamma sent everyone outside and locked the door. Putti began to weep loudly. Phaniyamma sat by her, and stroked her head. 'Putti, tell me now, do you want a male child or a female one?' In the midst of her pain, Putti said: 'I already have two girls, Phaniyamma. Wouldn't it be good to have a boy now? But I don't care as long as whatever's in my womb comes out.'

'All right. Listen to me and do what I say, and the child will be out in a trice.'

Phaniyamma turned the lantern flame higher. 'Now I'll

say the *mantra*, Putti. We'll tie a cloth round your eyes, and then you must take a deep breath. I'll tell you when.'

Premabai was mystified. She watched Phaniyamma tie the cloth round Putti's head, cut the lemon, stick it on the knife along with the turmeric root and the coal, swing it around Putti, and then put it down at her feet. Then she smeared oil all over her hands, and signalled to Premababi. 'Turn the child around by pressing the stomach, and I'll pull it out', she said. Premabai was astounded. Putti couldn't tell one from the other because of the blindfold. Both the Christian girl and the Brahmin widow had bare hands, and both wore white saris.

In a second, Phaniyamma's hand had turned the child gently inside the womb towards the vaginal opening. Premabai pushed from above.

'O Putti, take a deep deep breath now', said Phaniyamma. The child, a boy, came out easily. Premabai fell at Phaniyamma's feet.

Fifteen

Quickly wiping her hand on a piece of blanket, Phaniyamma removed Putti's blindfold. Putti's face was pouring with sweat even in that cold weather. Swabbing her face, Phaniyamma said: 'So you son's out, after having given you so much trouble. Now your mother-in-law will take care of you. Let me open the door.' By this time the baby was howling. Premabai had already cut the umbilical cord, bathed the child in warm water, and got rid of the refuse.

The household was delighted. Phaniyamma's *mantra* had done the trick. 'This Premabai's a chit of a girl who's never had or raised a baby herself. What's the matter with the government that they send people like her as midwives?' said the men sitting outside.

Phaniyamma had whispered in Premabai's ear not to tell anyone the truth. As she came out of the room, she said, raising her voice, 'So we'll be off then. This poor girl had a very hard time getting the child out. Give her something before she goes.'

The men were reluctant to pay. 'It was your *mantra* that did it, Phaniyamma. What did *she* do?' said Putti's father-in-law. The boatmen, who had rowed back and forth four times, sat waiting on the verandah for the two annas due to them. Seizing their chance, they said, 'Ayya, give us our two annas. We have to take these people across once more. Look how strong the current is.'

Quickly, Tippa Jois responded: 'You . . . And you're always asking for betelnut and leaf and tobacco. Do you think that doesn't cost anything? Go on, take these women back. On the day of the christening, we'll give you all a good meal.'

Phaniyamma was disgusted by his callousness. 'Come on, Sanka, come on, Budda. You too, Premabai, it's late. I'll get my brother Krishna to give you some money. Maybe these people don't have any money at home. Let's not sit and argue. I'd just gone down to the river to bathe, and my family might think I've been washed away. Come on, we must go now.'

On hearing Shanbhag Kittappa's name, Tippa Jois was alarmed. Knowing for certain that he would be roundly reprimanded next time he went to ask Kittappa a favour, Tippa Jois said quickly: '*Cheh*! what are you saying, Phaniyamma? I was only joking. I'll go get the money.' Left with no choice, he took the key of the safe from his sacred thread and got out some coins for the boatmen. He counted out two annas each and went into the kitchen. His wife whispered in Phaniyamma's ear and asked whether it would be enough to give Premabai eight annas. Ancheyatthe was again upset, but she said, without showing it, 'The girl's come here in all this rain and storm. Anyone else would have demanded rice, coconuts, bananas and jaggery. Shouldn't you give her at least two rupees? If you have the money, give it to her. If not, I have some at home. It's a baby boy. If you don't have any sugar in the house, give those three at least a piece of jaggery each to sweeten their mouths.'

Premabai got her two rupees and some jaggery. Likewise the boatmen. When they climbed into the boat again, the rain fell harder. The two men put some tobacco in their mouths, and said, 'Lady Grandmother, without you we'd have got nothing today. In the summer they cross the river on the stones. In the monsoon, they'd rather swim across than pay. And they talk about some tobacco they gave us a long time ago, what kind of people are they?'

Premabai added: 'This is the last time I'll cross this river, Phaniyamma. I'm dying of the cold and they don't even give me a drop of coffee. If you hadn't been there today, they'd have treated me worse than a dog.'

Not wanting them to continue in this vein, Phaniyamma broke in: 'Yes, my girl. Not everyone's alike, and you have to get used to dealing with all sorts. Poor thing, why did you take up this job at this young age? Go and get married, then you'll get some experience.'

'Me? Lord, watching all these childbirths makes me not want to get married ever. I'll stay as I am.'

The boat had reached the *arali* tree. The roar of the river was overpowering. The Shanbhag's son Naga, having come in search of Phaniyamma, was standing under the tree, holding an umbrella. He could not understand why Phaniyamma had gone to Kuruvalli. Not willing to answer his questions, Phaniyamma said quickly: 'I'll come home after my bath and tell you all that happened. Don't stand here in the rain. Go on home.' The boy went off.

'I'll come to your house tomorrow, Phaniyamma', Premabai said. 'I have to visit Bangaramma.'

'Go on, girl. First change out of those wet clothes, and get your mother to make you some hot coffee. Look how wet you are! You can come to our house some other day.'

As she said this, Phaniyamma began to dip herself in the water, a hundred and eight dips in all.

By evening Ancheyatthe had told her story. But in front of Bangari and Savitri she did not mention assisting at the childbirth.

During Navaratri Bangaramma gave birth to her own child. And the girl Premabai came to help. It was a difficult birth, but she managed. It was only in this house and in one or two others that people thought of offering coffee to the midwife. She would also get five rupees as a fee, and in those days that was a large sum indeed.

One day Premabai had come to see her patient, who told her Ancheyatthe's life-story. The girl responded: 'I hope you won't mind my saying this. But our people don't have hearts as hard as yours. Just think of it! To shave the head of such a little girl and to starve her for the rest of her life! It's not like

79

that among us. If one husband dies, you're allowed to take another.'

The recuperating mother Bangaramma did not remain silent. She said, smiling, 'Premabai, each community has its own practices, girl. And how old are you? You've learned the skill of a midwife, but have you experienced life? Your Jesu has preached so wonderfully: don't torture animals, don't hurt anyone, help the poor. But can you people follow all his teachings? Doesn't the Lord give all kinds of grain and fruit and vegetables to human beings? Why then do you kill those poor sheep and chickens and eat them? Didn't your own Jesu tell you not to do that? Do sheep and chickens harm anyone? Why not kill the tiger, bear, lion, and snake instead?'

Premabai was barely seventeen. She did not really know very much about the Christian faith. She hadn't even read the Bible completely. Not knowing how to answer Bangari's question, she was confused. Ancheyatthe realised this, and said to Bangari, 'Enough of that, Bangari. Poor thing, she's still a child. People follow whatever customs they're used to. If you examine everything closely, all customs may be wrong. But does this stop people from following them?'

Premabai was silent. But Bangari spoke: 'That's not what I meant, Ancheyatthe. What do I care if they eat fowl or pig? But these people are coming to our villages and converting the lower castes and the untouchables to their faith.'

Premabai agreed that this was true. 'Phaniyamma, you're right. I don't really know my religion. I just follow whatever my family does. Bangaramma, you're not angry with me?' Bangari laughed. 'Ayyo, don't say a word. I said something only because you did. Our customs are for us, and yours for your people. What's wrong with that?'

Premabai went away. A month later, when she visited them again, she said to Bangari that she'd given up eating meat.

'Ayyo, girl', said Bangaramma. 'I was only joking. Why did you stop? Won't your mother scold you?'

'I don't know why I did that. I had meat curry a couple of times, and both times I threw up. I can't understand why. Now I can't bear to watch a chicken being killed. And mutton I can't stand either. So I've stopped eating meat.'

'You're a funny girl. But even giving up meat won't help you to become a brahmin.'

'No one will take me into your caste even if I want to join. My only comfort is that I'm not eating the flesh of a harmless creature.'

Premabai remained in Tirthahalli for many a year. She did not marry. Nor did she start eating meat again. When Acheyatthe set out for Hebbalige, no one understood why Premabai should weep so bitterly.

'I won't come to this town again, girl', said Phaniyamma. 'Why do you cry like that? Am I a kinswoman?'

Sixteen

No one understood why the old woman should say to Premabai that which she had not uttered to anyone in the family. But it came to pass that although Ancheyatthe lived for some more years she never left Hebbalige again. No one could know her mind. Now her elder brother's grandchildren lived in Hebbalige, tending the remaining land and garden. On arriving from Tirthahalli, Phaniyamma had said, 'From now on I'm not going anywhere, my children. I'll stay here as long as I live, although I can't work as much as I used to be able to. I never lived with my husband and raised a family, but I've seen the world. I've finished all the pilgrimages and vows of obedience and all that. I was born in this house. Now I've come here to die.'

Her nephew Kanti said, 'Atthe, this house is yours. Did we ever ask you to leave? You can stay here for another hundred years if you wish. You're no burden to anyone.'

'Rama Rama, a hundred years! I'll become like the Himalaya mountains—eternal, if that's all right with you.'

Although she said she couldn't work like she used to, she continued to bathe in the pool, to cook for everyone, to say her prayers, to meditate, to help with the mothers after childbirth.

In her long life she never once fell ill. She never seemed to tire of working, and served everyone without discriminating. She never asked for anything, and above all hated unnecessary talk or unwilling work. Her favourite was the discreet Banashankari, who was the only one who knew all about the Putta Jois–Subbi affair, Sinki's childbirth and

Putti's. But it was only many years after Phaniyamma's death that Banashankari revealed these secrets to her children.

Phaniyamma's brother Kittappa used to say now and then that another woman like her could not have been born in the Kaliyuga. 'No one could have lived the life she did. Not even in days of yore. Is there a story like hers in the Ramayana, the Mahabharatha or the Bhagavatha? She must have been a goddess born in this guise under the curse of a sage.'

Kittappa died before his sister did. When she heard the news, she did not shed a tear. In silence, she went for a dip in the pond, and sat with her eyes shut when she came back to the house. Kittappa's wife Akkamma, who had suffered her husband's sudden fits of temper for years and patiently borne him four children, had died just before him. 'Your mother is as loyal to her husband as Sita. I wonder why Krishna flies into these rages', Phaniyamma used to say to Banashankari. The old woman was perhaps not disturbed by her brother's death, because his wife had gone first.

Now Banashankari, Bangari and Savitri did not feel like visiting their mother's house. Their children and their brothers were all married now. Once this writer's family, then living in Mysore, was visited by someone from Hebbalige, who brought news of Phaniyamma. 'She's still there', they said, 'but much changed. Once a day she roams around the garden and in the nearby woods, has her daily bath, says her prayers, eats a banana, and then sits all day telling her beads. Doesn't speak to a soul. She's over a hundred already. Wonder how the Lord still dwells in that body.'

While nursing her daughters after their deliveries, Banashankari would tell them stories about Phaniyamma. These girls had also lived with Ancheyatthe for two or three years and listened to all her tales.

Two years later, the news of Phaniyamma's demise reached Mysore. Those who heard the news were upset. Someone who had lived such a pure life could not have died like everyone else. Six months later, a visitor arrived from the Malnad. The talk turned to Ancheyatthe's death, and the visitor filled in the details.

Phaniyamma had been her usual self on Dashami day. The following day had been the Monday of Vaikunta Ekadashi. She had bathed, cooked a meal and served the children, prepared a snack for all those who were fasting, and sat on a low stool to tell her beads in the yard—the same yard where she had spilled the *kumkum* and *arashina* before her husband's death. Because of Ekadashi, she had not even eaten her customary banana. She said to Ambacchi, her great-grand-niece, 'Tell those people to eat their snack. It's late already, the sun's above the wall. Why are they wasting time chatting?'

She drew lotuses with *rangoli* power in front of the *tulasi* plant, said her prayers, distributed pieces of banana to all the children, and said this fruit had been offered up to the Lord Krishna.

Phaniyamma took two spoons of *tirtha* and picked up her beads. This was a familiar sight for the others, who now sat down to their snack.

The household knew that Phaniyamma would pray until sundown. After eating their beaten rice, the men and women threw their banana leaves on the rubbish heap. Ambacchi cleaned the dining area with cowdung and then washed her hands. As she climbed the steps into the kitchen, Ancheyatthe seemed to be bent over the *tulasi*. The prayers had been said and the obeisance completed. Why was Ancheyatthe bowing again? Ambacchi came down the steps without putting down the tumbler she was holding.

Ambacchi was married, and had been once to her husband's house. 'Not even a year since you married', her mother had said. 'You shouldn't fast this time.' So she had eaten a proper meal and not the snack. Not knowing whether her touch would defile Ancheyatthe, she called out: 'Ancheyatthe, why are you lying down? Are you dozing?' The sun had moved. It was after midday. Now Phaniyamma had slipped down to the ground, and her head rested on the foot of the *tulasikatte*. A body shrivelled like a sparrow's. A white sari. And the beads in her hand.

In Phaniyamma's one hundred and twelve years of existence, the *tulasikatte* had to be rebuilt each year after the rains, which washed away the mud structure. The plant flourished in its hundredth incarnation. Even now the *tulasi* looked splendid with its decorations of flour powder. Ancheyatthe lay there as if asleep.

Ambacchi, alarmed, shouted for her mother and father. The father came running out, his nostrils full of snuff, not having taken any betel leaf and nut because he was fasting. With his wife's help, he pulled Phaniyamma's body to an upright position. It slipped back. Ancheyatthe's soul had flown away as lightly as cotton fluff. Her face was placid as usual. On that holy day her old life had ended.

The townspeople gathered. The family cried. They sang her praises. That evening four old Brahmins of Hebbalige carried the bier on which Phaniyamma lay huddled like a tiny swan.

People from all castes came weeping to the cremation ground. In a corner of the flower garden, they had picked a spot for her, and her great-grandson lit the funeral pyre. Phaniyamma's other relatives heard the news only months later.

Glossary

Amaldar: a local person holding an office or a commission.

aralu: parched grain, especially parched paddy or corn.

arati: sacred flame on a bronze dish, moved in a circular fashion around the face of a god or human.

atthe: aunt or mother-in-law, depending on context.

bhagavathar: a man who dramatises incidents from the Bhagavatha or other Puranas.

chhatra: a kind of public hall where marriages are held.

Deepavali: festival of lights, in honour of the Emperor Bali, in the month of Karthika.

dosa: a kind of pancake.

ekanada: single-stringed instrument used to maintain a note.

ekadashi: eleventh day of the waxing or waning moon on which Smarthas, Vaishnavas and Ramanujas fast and keep awake.

gotra: lineage, family.

Gaurihabba: a yearly festival in honour of the goddess Gauri.

Gowda: non-Brahmin chief officer of a village, though not as powerful as the Shanbhag.

happala, sandige, balaka: varieties of dried flour, rice and spices to be fried before eating.

harikathe: story of Vishnu or Krishna, related with music and song.

hurihittu: flour made of parched paddy.

Ishwaralinga: image representing Shiva in a temple.

kachche dhoti: cloth tied by men around the waist, passing between the legs.

kadubu: a kind of cake with a sweet filling, fried or steam-cooked.

Kailas: home of the god Shiva.

Kashiyatre: for the bridegroom, a 'pilgrimage' to indicate the completion of his studies. A ritual to dramatise the bringing back of the groom by the bride's people.

Malnad: the Western Ghats in Karnataka.

mandakki: puffed rice with split peas.

mangalasutra: necklace (of gold, black beads or just plain string) worn to indicate that a woman is married.

mora: a bamboo tray, for winnowing corn, etc. used for a variety of purposes.

mridanga: a kind of drum.

Mutt at Sringeri: established by Adi Sankaracharya. There are five such 'temples', including the ones at Sringeri and Dwarka.

panchagaya: five things obtained from the cow: milk, curds, ghee, urine and dung.

Patel: headman of a village.

prasada: food offered first to the gods and then to devotees.

Pushpaka: a kind of aeroplane used by King Ravana in the Ramayana.

rangoli: coloured flour-powder used to make auspicious patterns.

rupee, anna, pie: a rupee is equal to 16 annas, and one anna equal to 12 pice.

sandhyavandane: meditation and prayer rituals performed traditionally three times a day.

sankalke panje: a *madi* dhoti used on auspicious and religious occasions, later gifted to the poor.

sanyasi: ascetic, holy person.

Shanbhag: clerk or accountant of a village, usually a brahmin.

shavige: vermicelli made from rice or wheat.

taluk: geographical division of region, based on revenue collection.

tapasvini: a holy person continuing to live with the family, unlike the sanyasi or ascetic.

tirtha: a liquid offered first to the god and then by the spoonful to each devotee.

tulasikatte: sacred plant worshipped by Brahmins every day and also on special occasions.

turmeric-kumkum: yellow and red powder, considered auspicious, worn on forehead and base of neck (especially turmeric).

Ugadi: festival to celebrate the new year according to the lunar calendar.

upanayana: investiture or thread-ceremony for a Brahmin boy.

vrata: vows of obedience.

*

Season and Months in the Lunar Calendar

Vasantha ritu: Chaitra, Vaishakha (March, April).

Greeshma ritu: Jyeshtha, Aashaada, Vaishakha (May, June).

Varsha ritu: Shravana, Bhaadrapada (July, August).

Sharad ritu: Ashwayuja, Karthika (September, October).

Hemantha ritu: Margashira, Pushya (November, December).

Shishira ritu: Magha, Phalguna (January, February).

*

Note: The Western calendar months coincide only approximately.

*

Note: At the present time (1991) there are approximately 28 rupees to the pound sterling.